The Last HORIZON

anthony hartig

The Earth is the cradle of humanity, but mankind cannot stay in the cradle forever.

Konstantin Tsiolkovsky

The Last Horizon copyright © Anthony Hartig

First Edition

All rights reserved.

ASIN: B00AI2TZE2

ISBN-13: 978-1481038249
ISBN-10: 1481038249

Printed in the United States of America

10 9 8 7 6 5 4 3 2

for

Jassie
A real tough chick
I love you girlie

Chapter 1

Nikki

I think back to the evening it started at Kurlie's place-- Curly's Tavern. A dingy, soot-stained brick structure lost among the third rate pawn shops, liquor stores, and low cost flats in a forgettable district populated by cut-throat hustlers and pushers after sundown. Not the kind of place a stranger wants to be caught alone in unless you were armed or known by the locals. Me? Well I'm not a local, but I've been here enough times for the urchins to be familiar with my face and reputation.

I adjusted my fedora, and zipped-up my leather jacket to conceal the shoulder holster that housed my Cobalt as I crossed the boulevard and zeroed-in on the saloon. The late afternoon shadows grew long on the streets and I could hear the heavy rhythm of a synthesized bass drum seeping through the heavy double doors of Curly's as I drew closer. The repetitious beat seemed so prevalent in every techno-pop push song; a heavy thump that seemed to shift your bones to the left when your brain is stewed on cheap beer accented by the flavor of flat cheese crackers and bland cold cuts.

The foyer was darkened by one of Kurlie's oversized bouncers, a man that had a head the size of a grapefruit and shoulders as wide as a Knifeball offensive lineman. He grunted at me in recognition as I entered the pub and continued to scan the boulevard with a suspicious eye.

You can never be too careful in my line of work, and I always packed heat whenever I ventured into a deal. I swore to myself that I'd never step foot in this hole again, but Kurlie's message the other day got my curiosity up when he said he would make it worth my while, "...an offer you can't refuse, Nikki, but I can't hold it open for ya long." was the way he phrased it, and what the hell, I needed the gig and the money for the upkeep of my ship.

So against my better judgment, I found myself at Curly's pushing through the multi-colored strobe lights filtered through the haze of stale cigarette smoke. The club was slowly filling up with the silhouettes of baggy-eyed working stiffs, cycle gang members, and questionable characters nursing their watered-down cocktails.

"Nikki! How ya been, hon?" A gravelly voice cut through the din of happy hour. It was Kira, a cocktail waitress in her early forties that had too much class to be in a place like this. She balanced a tray of beer mugs over her left shoulder with the grace of a dancer as she leaned over the mahogany counter and shouted over the music to the bartender.

"Charlie, I'm going to need two Aftermaths and a Kidney Punch for table three, and we need to cut-off the ass monkey at table twelve. I swear, if he grabs my butt again and asks to be breast fed I'm going to open his head with the pitcher on his table."

Kira sighed as she set down the tray on the bar and gave me a hug. "Wow, look at you! My Nikki getting more devastating every day!"

"Kira, you look wonderful," I beamed as I hugged her back hard. She was like a big sister to me, "How's it shakin', crazy lady?"

"Aw, you know," she put an arm around my shoulder and kissed my forehead, "workin' my butt off and keepin' the dream alive as best I can." Kira smiled as she wiped her hands on her apron.

"Kurlie here?"

"His usual place." Kira motioned toward the back of the room. "Here on business, huh?"

"Well I didn't come here for a free pelvic exam."

"HA! HA!" Kira snorted as she shook her head. "You're such a paper cut!"

"I better get going and get this over with." I sighed as I scanned the dance floor for a path."

"Okay," Kira grinned, "but be careful Red Riding Hood, the wolves are out in full force tonight."

"Nice seeing you again, Kira."

"Take care of yourself, hon." Kira embraced me again. "You stay out of trouble, okay girl?"

"You too crazy lady."

As I made my way through the crowd, a heavyset barfly with a sculptured goatee stepped in front of me--the jerk from table twelve.

"Well hallo there sweet cheeks. You sure are a tiny little thing." He leered as he began to undress me with his bloodshot eyes. His breath reeked of alcohol as he leaned into my face. "How 'bout you let me take you home and show ya a good time?"

This guy must have outweighed me by two hundred pounds. "How 'bout you fragg-off, fat boy?" I scowled as I side-stepped him. By then, some of the barstool occupants elbowed each other and smiled as they turned their attention to the unfolding drama.

"Whoa! Whoa! You've got a smart mouth lady," he grinned as he put his hand on my shoulder, "I like it when they talk dirty and play hard to get. Wadda say you let big daddy show ya what a magnificent pagan beast I can be?" He smirked and licked his lips as he stared at my breasts.

"You looking to dance, big guy?" I smiled shyly as I squared-off in front of him.

"I'm looking to unload." He swayed as he nonchalantly brushed the left side of his jacket open and exposed an unbuttoned shirt that revealed his hairy chest. I knew it; low forehead, protruding eyebrow ridge, and thinks with his crotch--Neanderthal man.

"Come on, baby, let me top-off your gas tank." He stuck out his thick gray tongue and wiggled it at me.

"Let's dance, handsome." I said demurely as I puckered and blew him a kiss.

"Now that's more like it!" He smiled broadly as he puckered-up and leaned down into my face.

I reached up seductively, put my right hand behind his head, and pulled him down hard and fast as I rammed my left elbow into the scumbag's nose with a sharp smack and followed through with two fast jabs to the face. His head snapped back as he put his hands over his nose and blood flowed between his fingers.

"YAAAH! Farking slag!" He slurred through split lips as he staggered sideways.

"All you can handle "Big Daddy"." I growled as I sprang forward and threw a side kick with my left leg into his stomach.

"OOOPHF!" He grunted as he wheeled backwards through the crowd, crashed into some tables at the edge of the dance floor, and scattered chairs and their occupants into the darkness.

The crowd parted as I walked calmly to where he lay crumpled on the sticky film on the floor composed of wasted beer, liquor, and now, blood. "You should learn to pay your respects." I glared over the wheezing mound of fractured alpha male. "In case you're wondering, the name's Wells...Nikki Wells, and you've just been chicked."

I tipped my hat and bowed politely at the crowd as they applauded, whistled, and cat-called to show their appreciation for the sideshow. I saw Kira at the front of the pack. She grinned and gave me a thumbs-up, and I continued my journey through the crowded dance floor.

I spotted Kurlie in a back booth with a curvy blonde half his age sitting on his lap. She was wearing a very short black strapless dress. He waved me to his table, and even through the noise of underground pop, I could hear his deep, raspy laugh as he leaned into the blonde with a sinister Cheshire grin that meant no good but at the very least promised a vexing conversation laced with perverse humor.

The girl, as if on cue, stood up with a polite smile and dismissed herself at my approach as Kurlie winked and motioned for me to take the seat across from him.

"Nikki, nice moves back there with that clown." Kurlie clapped with approval as he shook his head and puffed on his cigar.

I haven't seen Kurlie in almost a year, but he was one of those people that never seemed to age. Heavy-set with a bald head, he was a man in his fifties with a powerful build that he liked to cloak in expensive suits.

"Sorry about the mess, Kurl."

"Forget about it. A little dinner theater is good for business." Kurlie beamed as he exhaled a thick plume of smoke. "Been a while, no? How ya been?"

"Not too bad, Kurlie. Still going after the young ones, eh?" I nodded my head in the direction that the blonde had vanished.

"Every chance I get." Kurlie winked. "You're looking really fine this evening, young lady. Love the hat. So when are you gonna let me buy you some dinner, Nikki?"

"Down boy," I smiled as I settled into my chair, "and save the charm for the bimbo. I see you've got a new man at the door. What happened to Gus?"

"A little mishap last week, he's getting some dental work done and will be out for a few weeks." Kurlie shrugged. "Punctual as always, Nikki. That's what I always liked about you--always on time."

"Well I'm glad there's something you like about me, Kurlie, because there's absolutely nothing I like about you."

"Heh-heh-heh!" Kurlie chuckled, "That's my girl, always kiddin' around. Hey, why don't 'cha have a drink? It's on the house."

"I'll pass, Kurlie," I said sternly. "Whatever deal you're about to propose I'd better damn well be sober."

"Oh come on now, Nikki, would ol' Kurl steer ya wrong?"

"Absolutely."

"Oh stop, I'm starting to get giddy with all the flattery."

"Want to get down to business, Kurlie?"

"All right, just cool your jets for a minute." Kurlie grinned as he laced his fingers together and cracked his knuckles. "Ya know where Medusa's set?"

"Yeah, it's a star neighboring Polaris isn't it?"

"Lemme get the chart out." Kurlie replied patiently as he pulled out a star map and unfolded it onto the table. "The third planet around Medusa is Nexus," Kurlie said dryly as he put his index finger on the satellite, "it's settled by miners and deep space colonists. There are several colonies concentrated around the base of a mountain range called Sertina's Pass."

"I can also see that it's a pretty good distance from here." I squinted as I traced the distance from Earth to Nexus on the chart with my index finger.

"Sure is. The fastest growing city that's significant to all the Sertina colonies is Fluture. Your destination. Can that Zephyr of yours hold a thirty-five thousand pound cargo?"

"Depends on what it is."

"Wadda you care, Nikki? The trip's illegal anyway. Since the conflict with the Serenian Empire has escalated again, there are no solo flights allowed outside the solar system."

"I don't haul weapons or drugs, you know that."

"Now would I be mixed up in weapons or drugs?"

"Up to your ass."

"Heh-heh-heh!" Kurlie shook his head, "There's that sense of humor again." He grinned as he took a sip of his drink. "No, nothing like that, Nikki."

"No contraband, Kurlie."

"Contraband." Kurlie chortled. "What's contraband? Everything's contraband to somebody some where. Besides, this is just stuff for the ladies."

"What do you mean?"

"Like I said, Nexus is just getting settled and it's a wild, wild place. Lots of drinking and gambling. A bunch of mining colonies on the frontier and the settlers have their wives and girlfriends with 'em. The cargo I need ya to take is stuff for the ladies--fancy soaps, powders, and lipstick. You know, things you ladies just have to have."

"That's contraband."

"Sure, sure, but it's nice harmless contraband, Nikki, you can go check it out for yourself on the docks."

"So what's the split?"

"Fifty-fifty, girlie, for four mil."

"I...what? Two large? "

"Ya heard me. Fifty-fifty. And four large *is* your cut."

"Oh boy, what's the catch? Nobody pays that kind of money to move cosmetics across space."

"No catch, the split is right down the middle. Four million. I just need you to make the drop ASAP. That, and I wanna send an envoy along for the ride to make sure the goods get in the right hands on time."

"An envoy?"

"Yeah, an escort for the product if you will. You get him to Nexus and back and that's it."

"Kurlie, you know I work alone. No passengers."

"It's just one guy. Name's Fenmore Scott. He knows Nexus like the back of his hand. Besides, it's always good to buddy-up with someone on these voyages, no? He's part of the deal."

"Kurlie..."

"Hey! Speak of the devil." Kurlie smiled as he stood up and waved to a well dressed man working his way through the crowd toward us. "There he is now. You're gonna love this guy..."

Fenmore

I woke up this morning on shaky legs; wobbling down the stairs with fog in my head--nauseous, and on the verge of having an out-of-body experience triggered by my hangover. I could still see the pools of blood from the night before. Even as I mixed a vodka and milk breakfast I could hear the sound of gunfire and still see the plumes of my breath absorbed into the darkness.

Last night, while watching a funny movie on the telecom and not holding anything in particular in my mind, I heard the screech of tires, the thump of meat being slapped hard, and the thrashing of some terrible beast on the porch.

When I parted the curtains and looked out my grimy window, there was a buck--an eight pointer, spewing blood from post to post on my front porch, kicking and bleeding, he was in shock and stopped only for a second or two as if he were transmitting a message for salvation as he looked at me with his marble-black eyes.

Transmitted or not, I understood. I backed away from the glass, and ran and grabbed a pistol that I had stashed between the couch cushions. Barefooted and drunk, I ran up front and put one into his head. I went back inside to call the sheriff but the phone was already ringing.

"Sir, we just received a call from a motorist and we understand a deer has been hit on your street. We've dispatched an officer to come and put it down."

"I've done that already."

"You've..."

"Yes. Somehow it ended up on my front porch. You'll have to send someone from the Department of Sanitation instead."

"Yes sir. We'll have a clean-up crew out within the hour."

"Thanks."

Going to bed seemed the next best thing to do, so off I went. One thing that can be had by living out next to the woods that one can't get within town limits, is privacy. For this I am grateful. I don't like questions and I never have. Neighbors like to ask questions and I don't want to be bothered. I don't like dealing with the reciprocating ratios of self-disclosure.

Out here, the houses are not real close together and the main road is just offset from my property for convenience. The beauty of it is that the road is concealed by a grove of birch trees and shrubs.

Neighbors. Walter and Sandy live next door with their three kids; two from this marriage who are twins, a boy and girl of eleven years, and an older girl from Sandy's previous marriage who is starting to drive now. I don't really know them, but the kids tromp about the yard hip deep in snow--they are intrepid and determined in the face of northern winters.

Yesterday when I was home drinking a vodka and lemonade, I heard a huge chunk of ice fall from the roof. Nothing for more than a second or two when I heard a thumping against the wall of the house. I went to investigate and found the younger girl's legs poking out of a snow pile by the back door. Pulling her out was a lot easier than trying to get her to stop crying, and the whole scene would have been a disaster had Sandy not come out to help.

I'm really not cut-out for this savior shit, and honestly, someone should have been watching this mouse. I see them though, trudging through the snow, trooping out after their dog who's constantly whiffing for winter berries on frozen branches.

Renting them the house was a good idea and here's why: when I moved out here for good I didn't look for work. I didn't make my source of income known to anyone, and that's the way I like it. But I almost forgot that small town people are nosy. They love to gossip, and someone in the area who cannot be identified as working there is definitely an outsider. The subject of gossip and speculation.

I wanted to blend in, so I bought the house next door, rented to a nice family, and sent the money to the bank regularly. I kept my other finances separate from the local financial institution.

The truth is I don't have to work. Not now. Not ever if I live as I have been--modestly and well within my means. But from my personal history, work is all I have. It's all I know. It's actually who I am.

I know what it means to look back centuries on the legions of soldiers that marched into battle and said the ominous words from the Hindu scripture Bhagavad Gita: "I am become death, the destroyer of worlds." Even as late as this war with the Serenians, the phrase is written on the backs of tactical helmets and body armor of grunts in the field...and so the tattoo of death remains unchanged to present day.

I am become drunk. That is what I know today. I am become vodka. Perhaps that's a better way to put it. There's a mil-spec assault shotgun in the bathroom and one by the door. I keep a Raven automatic pistol stashed in the couch cushions in the living room where I sit and watch the endless parade of interstellar news on a split-screen telecom. I keep a 24 hour clock on the wall so I know if it's night or day. I'm often confused about if I need a drink or if I've just had one.

The groceries are delivered twice a week by a faded yellow and silver hovering automaton from the local chain so I don't have to drive to town and interact with human beings. My list never changes from white bread, liquor, hamburger and eggs, some milk for my morning cocktail, and some lemonade for the afternoons if my stomach can take it.

Mostly though, the mystery of why my useless life is guarded with such energy is in fact a mystery to me as well. I have not produced anything of value in this life. I am a sociopath. I killed small animals as a boy and I've gone on to kill humans with frightening efficiency in the service of the military. To my understanding, my extraction from combat years ago was fast and covert.

I don't remember much, the Alliance found my body crushed and half dead. It took a year, and the surgeons thought my recovery a miracle. So here I am, reconstructed and released as Fenmore Scott.

If by elimination a man can contribute to the sum of things, then show me the math. Here's the real rub: now, with drink and sloth, I have drifted aimlessly into alcoholism. I stagger around in my fart smelling sweats, a hairless ape with some education and two biomechanical legs and a left bio-mech arm that can punch a hole through a concrete wall.

All this hardware cognitively integrated and sheeted with layers of synthetic tissue and epidermal membrane. They look and feel so real, and sometimes I forget that I'm a host to interlocking cybernetic neuro-transmitters and silicone micro-implants. I am become bionic.

Picture the scene of the neighbor's child trapped beneath a hundred plus pounds of snow and ice. Her rescuer, drunk with a beard crusted stiffly with dried drool, stinking of a month without a bath; stumbling, and wheezing; unsteadily opens the door to discover tiny feet sticking out of a snowbank; yanking unceremoniously on the limbs he extracts the terrified child, who in red-faced fear leaps from him into the arms of her mother.

This is the beast I have become. Once sinew and the cat paw of death, now the soiled and malodorous sloth of number 1650, Route #28 in the little hamlet of North River. Were it not for my cat Damn it, who refuses to acknowledge me anyways, no one needs me, remembers me, or sends an awful fruitcake at Christmas.

The one thing that I have done besides remove my tumorous self from the body of society, the one thing I can say I've accomplished in my forty-six years on the planet, is pull an eleven year old from the snow.

My money, my position and rank in the military, and my love for Mozart and appreciation of Degas in the overall scheme of things will mean nothing. When death comes to call, I'll end and that's it. I'll become protein; eaten like a shark eats a walrus. No soundtrack. No chorus of angels, last rites, or ceremony. Gone.

"Here lies Fenton Scott--goddamn he was a drunk." Perhaps there's some dignity in it that way. How bad can it be to almost instantly be transformed into food? Enter the ecosystem in the fast lane.

I staggered by a room upstairs that I like to call my library. Inside on a desk, the computer light of the monitor blinks and the cruel process of apathy and neglect take over in my mind.

A question forms: "Do I bother answering the call?" It's by computer that I receive and accept my contracts. Long years have gone since I've accepted a contract to kill anyone. Long years since I was in any shape to do so.

Since no one has seen me in ages, and since I don't go out or attend anything like a social function, no one knows I'm an enormous turd. So the calls come, usually months apart, but they are something I get with regularity.

Anyway, they come without a ribbon or bow, they come without warning through a scrambled network disguised as a news site called "The Daily", but they always come with money. Lots of money.

Waking up in my chair downstairs is not an occurrence that is rare or in the least bit foreign to me, and I know by the pinch in my bladder that I've been here a while. Getting up to take a leak, I stumble, reel, and I put my socked foot into a bowl of wet cat food.

"Damn it! Fugg...grrr...damn it!"

The cat flattens herself with gleaming eyes, then blasts-off the couch and bolts upstairs to hide. She knows it's not her, and I never mess with her, but the noise has set her into rocketship mode.

After pissing, I navigate the stairs to look for my pet and see the blinking light of the computer set to a constant green. That's funny, I don't remember answering it. But I've answered it though, or it wouldn't be solid green. Had I ignored the message, it would either go on blinking red or disappear after a while. A short while. But it's not. It's green. Solid. Staring at me with one cycloptic eye, it draws me into the library.

Oh boy. No really...oh boy! I think I'm in some trouble. You just don't answer a call like that and not follow through, and following through is not my specialty lately. For a year and a half I've been in the woods; I invited and allowed the fates to take a great big dump on me...a billowy, blustering, steaming pile of poo on my life. Now I've done something to alter being a bystander. What the hell do I do now?

Okay, okay, okay. First thing's first. Check the message. Remain calm and read it. I sat down at the desk and slowly hit the Enter key on the board and a blue dossier screen popped up with instructions after I typed in my password.

The profile was a bald, heavy-set man that resided on a planet called Nexus. Robert Charon, age 54. Suspected of heading a slavery and prostitution ring, he was also mixed up with the manufacturing and distribution of crunch dust. Planet of origin, Earth.

This guy was always one step ahead of the law and a real piece of work: busted for armed robbery and assault with a deadly weapon at age 14, authorities believe Charon's indoctrination into the life involved cleaning-out the register of a local holograph and music store at gunpoint.

He shot a customer that tried to run out of the building. A lady in her third trimester. She lost her baby from the trauma. Charon fled on foot with a bag full of money and credits but was picked up by the cops four days later when an anonymous source dimed his whereabouts for a reward.

Charon was out in under two years because he was a minor. But while in stir, it was believed that he shanked two kids, but it could never be proven. The story is that Charon stabbed the other two inmates while they tried to rape another young man that was just brought into the facility the night before.

23

Turns out that the kid he saved was the only son of a known syndicate boss named Jonathan Ness. A major player in the underground and deemed untouchable by the Alliance Council. So Charon had achieved status from the other juveniles on the inside for his actions, and inadvertently paved the way for his future by saving Ness's son.

They became friends, and that friendship blossomed when they were released. Ness's kid, Fredric, introduced Charon to his old man as a gesture.

Years later, at the tender age of 24, the police nailed Charon for carjacking, but he beat the rap and never served time thanks to a high priced lawyer provided by his new fairy godfather Jonathan Ness. Ness became his benefactor, and two years later, when his own son overdosed on a harquinol and crunch dust cocktail called a speed demon, he took Charon under his wing like a son.

At age 32, Charon was suspected of kidnapping an 18 year old girl along with multiple homicides that occurred across three cities over a period of four years...all believed to have been done on behalf of his newly adopted family. He had graduated to hitman. But the authorities couldn't pin any of the murders on him, and the girl was never found.

He turned up later on Nexus as the "Manager" of the largest casino on Colony-9 (also known as Fluture). Nothing slipperier than a criminal that migrates across planets and colonies.

For Charon, money would never be a problem. When his mentor Ness died, Charon was rooted deep in the family business. A made man. He had expensive tastes and apparently enjoyed indulging in the finer things in life. Well-manicured, well-dressed, and heavily guarded by a group of scumbags wearing pricey suits, it just goes to show you that no matter how many times you polish a turd, it's still a turd.

The profile indicated that Charon was behind the kidnapping of young women, getting them addicted to crunch, and turning them into high dollar call girls for the big spenders in his casino. Politicians, corporate shakers, celebrities, and inter-planetary delegates...a nice long roster of wealthy clients. All hush-hush and stealth for the reputations on the make.

I may not have amounted to much in the eyes of many in this life, but at least I've never preyed on the innocent. Charon was a predator of women and children. A reptile. And now my employers want him dead, and I'm the one that gets to end him for a twelve million credit contract. I am become death.

The instructions: get to New Detroit within the next two weeks and find a man named Charles "Kurlie" Montrell, a mid-level crime boss. He would provide me with a means to get to Nexus undetected. An expense account has been set up for my mission. But the first move--get sober...

Chapter 2

Kurlie

This outsider walks into my bar a few weeks ago. Overdressed for my place, and that's what made him stand out a little. Looked more like one of those stuck-up uptown residents. His face, voice, and name weren't familiar, so my man at the door, Gus, stops and leans on him for information before allowing him inside. What a mess that turned out to be for Gus.

I didn't see it happen, but from what some of my customers told me, this guy basically turned Gus' face inside-out; people screaming over the music and running out of the saloon in a panic...like I said, what a mess. Bad for business too.

Who the hell was this guy to come to my tavern and start breaking arms? I smelled a set-up, undercover cops were slick, but this guy reeked Federation as he walked across the dance floor and made his way to my table. My guys stepped in front of him but I signaled them to step aside and let him through. I was curious about this insect and I wanted a closer look.

"Mr. Montrell?" The stranger asked evenly as he side-eyed my men.

"Who wants to know, Billy badass?" I inquired as I lit a cigar and exhaled.

"May I have a few minutes of your time? I promise to make it worth your while."

I nodded and the man pulled out a chair across from me and sat down. He adjusted the lapels on his suit and folded his hands on the table as he cleared his voice. He had one of those carpethead flattop haircuts that Feds always had. Nice suit, bad haircut.

"Mr. Montrell, I can't begin to express my gratitude for allowing me to have this audience with you."

"Gratitude? You left my man at the door face down and scared the hell out of all my clients. You're costing me a lot of money and now I need a new doorman."

"You're right Mr. Montrell. Please accept my sincerest apologies for stirring-up such an unsavory scene." The stranger gestured calmly. "But your man tried to raze me when I tried to get into your establishment. I had no choice but to defend myself."

This guy was a smooth talker. Calm. He made me nervous and his vocabulary made him sound like he had a stick up his ass. "What do you want Mr...."

"Scott. Fenmore Scott. I've been told that you're a man that can make things happen."

"Perhaps. But I'll tell you what I can make happen, Mr. Scott. You can stand up and walk out of here under your own power, or my employees can help you out of here under mine. I don't think you'll like the second option. *That's* something that I can make happen."

Four of my men had positioned themselves behind the stranger to flank him. I sat with my hands flat on the table facing Scott, wondering how he was able to take down Gus at the door so quickly.

"Well before anybody does anything they'll regret," the stranger stated grimly, "I need for something to happen. I need a favor, Mr. Montrell." Scott smiled. "I need your help."

"Help doing what?"

"I need to get to Nexus for a few days. Business. Then I want to come back home. I understand that you may be able to make this happen."

I started laughing. This guy was funny. My men began laughing with me. This man was a fool. A dead fool.

"Don't know what you're talking about Mr. Scott. Take a look around you. I'm a business man not a travel agent. All I am is the proprietor of this gentleman's bar. Besides, you're talking about an making an illegal flight outside the solar system. I don't like trouble, and you're trouble. So if you'll excuse me, my coworkers will now escort you out of my establishment--under my power." I nodded and smiled, and two of my men stepped forward and grabbed this Fenmore Scott by the arms.

It happened so fast. I barely had time to blink when he sprung out of his seat, and the next thing I know, both of my men were on the floor and their teeth were embedded in the tabletop with splashes of blood. Scott had disarmed my third bodyguard when he snapped his arm, struck him across the neck, and left him gurgling under a table in a crumpled ball gasping for air.

My last gunman tried to shoot him, but Scott was fast enough to close the distance between them and threw a left jab to my man's jaw that connected with a devastating smack that instantly shattered his face and rendered him unconscious before he hit the ground. This all happened in a span of less than five seconds.

Scott sighed as he picked up one of my guy's pistols and set it on my table. He wasn't even breathing hard.

I sat calmly shaking my head. "Very impressive. You know, Mr. Scott, those were some of my best men."

"If you say so."

"Heh-heh-heh! Who the hell are you?" I demanded as I glanced at the bloody teeth stuck on the edge of the table.

"I'm the one that can change your life forever, Mr. Montrell." Scott glared as he reached into his jacket and threw down several stacks of money on the table. "There's one million. Get me to Nexus within two weeks with no questions asked, and you get another million when I get back. It's easy money and the people that I work for will appreciate your cooperation."

"And who do you work for?"

"Do this and opportunity will knock on your door again. No questions. Do we have a deal?" Scott asked coldly.

"Do I have a choice?"

"Everyone's got choices, Mr. Montrell. I hope you make the right one."

"Well then, I guess we have a deal, Mr. Scott. How will I get a hold of you when I arrange for your transport?"

"I'll contact you."

"When?"

Scott didn't answer. He smiled callously, turned around, and walked out of my bar. I motioned for my bartender to come to my table.

"Yeah, boss?"

"Get a tail on him. Find out where he's staying and keep an eye on him until I figure out the next move, and have Tommy the geek do a check. I want to know everything we can find out about this guy. I want to know where he came from and what he wants with Nexus. I want to know who I'm doing business with."

"Yes boss."

"No one pays two million to go to Nexus. Also, get Nikki Wells on the line."

"Yes boss."

Fenmore

I staked-out the tavern every night; sitting at different tables observing the regulars and memorizing the lay-out of the establishment. This was definitely a working man's slab, lots of leather and faded denim--faded like the weathered statues that wore them; men who's faces were carved in stone like their fates.

Montrell sat at the same table every night surrounded by his henchmen and was visited by an assortment of characters throughout the evening. Some of his guests were older and seemed to have a dignified air about them, but I could surmise from their entourage of bodyguards that they were members of some of the city's crime families. Montrell was connected, a ruthless up and coming boss who was getting attention in underground circles for his reputation for getting things done. It was obvious this club was just a cover for something bigger operating beneath the surface.

The first time I saw Ms. Wells she was wearing a slightly oversized leather bomber jacket and a black fedora. Very retro, and the jacket was a good way to conceal the Cobalt automatic she carried in the shoulder holster. She didn't dress like a typical pilot, but then again, what would I know about the younger generation. Nikki also wore heavy eyeliner and tight black leather pants and cowboy boots that made her look like she was fronting a neo-techno punk band.

She was undoubtedly attractive, a petite brunette with a look of innocence that was out of place in this environment, but judging from the clientele's reaction to her as she made her entrance, she was known by most in this locale.

What I caught me off guard was the way she handled herself when someone more than twice her size physically tried to intimidate her; she defended herself in a manner that indicated training in close quarter combat. The moves she executed were precise and deadly. Not the kind taught in some woman's self-defense course, but the kind that required study and discipline.

As I made my way to Montrell's table I could see that she was engaged in an argument with him about taking along a passenger to Nexus...me.

Nikki

"**N**ikki, I'd like you to meet an acquaintance of mine." Kurlie grinned as he gestured for the stranger to sit down with us. "Fenmore Scott, this is Nikki Wells. The pilot that will get you to Nexus. Nikki, this is Fenmore Scott. Your passenger."

I eyed Scott as I shook his hand and sat back down. "A pleasure Mr. Scott."

"Likewise Ms. Wells." Scott replied coyly.

There was something a little off with this Scott character. After a few minutes of small talk, it dawned on me what it was that bothered me about this guy...Scott wasn't one of Kurlie's goons. The way he scanned his surroundings implied that he was unfamiliar with this environment. He wasn't one of Kurlie's henchmen.

"Okay, Kurlie," I resigned as I stared into his eyes hard for a sign of deception, "I think we may have ourselves a deal."

"Hey, great!" Kurlie's smile widened as he clapped his hands together.

"When do you need me to leave?"

"Tonight. The cargo's already being loaded into you ship."

"What? Tonight?" I gasped in shock.

"Well it better be tonight, you're due to set down in Nexus no later than the 24th."

"24th of what?"

"24th of this month."

"Of this month? Kurlie, that's in six days!"

"Well, six-and-a-half if you include tonight."

"Have you lost your mind? Look at the chart! Kurlie, you see how far Nexus is--it's over three parsecs!" I spouted and pointed at the map. "There's no way I could cover this distance in six days. This trip will take six weeks."

"Oh come on, Nikki, you know how to get there in six days."

"How?"

"All's ya have to do is go through the Pipe."

"Ooooh, I see. *That's* the catch."

"Why, what's wrong? Now don't tell me you're scared of the Pipe."

"I'm scared out of my wits. Deal's off, Kurl. Sorry Mr. Scott, you'll need to find another flight to Nexus."

"What's the matter, Nikki?" Kurlie grunted with dismay.

"I'm not doing it. I'm not going through the Pipe. Forget it. No way!" I got up from the table shaking my head in disdain as I began to walk away.

"Is there a problem Mr. Montrell?" Scott glared at Kurlie.

"No, no," Kurlie reassured Scott as he stood up, "I've got this under control." Kurlie grinned. "Geez, I thought you were a real space jockey, Nikki. If someone would've told me that Nikki Wells had that little streak of yellow down her back, I never would've believed it."

"Don't try to get a rise out me, Kurlie. I'm not yellow, I'm smart. It's not gonna happen. I'll see you around."

"Make it around eight o'clock. That's as long as I can hold the job open."

"Goodbye Kurlie."

"Hey don't go away mad, Nikki, it'll just make it harder for ya to come back."

"I'm not coming back!" I barked as I headed for the door.

Who did I think I was fooling anyway? I'm a smuggler, a space tick, and that's all there is to it. I'm a runner and I'm damned good at it. I've taken some major risks over the years, but somehow or another the Federation never caught up with me. Sure there have been some close calls, and I'll even admit I got a cheap thrill from being chased by patrols through asteroid fields, but they never got close enough to I.D. the Zephyr.

I was reckless and driven by bravado back then, and to a large extent, the romantic notion of establishing a reputation among the rest of the runners; or at least to having bragging rights for my misadventures or exaggerated versions of them in dives like Curly's Tavern.

When I got home I grabbed the basics and stuffed them into my flight bag. The Cobalt was secured in its shoulder holster along with extra clips on my belt. A couple of other things I like to carry on my voyages were throwing spikes tucked in an ankle wrap, a tactical knife sheathed in my belt, and titanium razor knots mounted on a six foot whip disguised as a leather belt. A girl's got to be prepared.

I put on my flight suit and grabbed a spare that had been hanging in my closet for ages. The suit belonged to another pilot I used to mess around with until he disappeared over a year ago. To this day I still don't know what happened to him.

There were rumors floating around that his ship was hijacked during his last run, but nobody knows for sure. It hurts my heart when I think of him and look at the small holograph of us together. I miss his smile and voice.

I packed a small bag, double-checked my shoulder holster and Cobalt before putting on my bomber jacket, and checked myself in the mirror one more time before putting on my hat. I had a cab drive me down to the launch port where my ship was docked.

When I arrived at the Inter-port, Scott was waiting at the entrance wearing a flannel jacket. All he carried was a duffle bag and a backpack slung over one shoulder.

"Good evening, Mr. Scott." I smiled.

"You can call me Scotty." He replied dryly. "And good evening to you too, Ms. Wells."

"Nikki." I nodded. "Here, I brought this for you." I handed Scott the flight suit. "It looks like your size. You're going to need it for the voyage. They've got lockers in the hanger where you can change."

"Thank you."

"We'd better get inside and get this clambake underway."

"Okay."

"Let me do the talking." I said firmly as I picked up my bag.

We walked casually through the hanger with our gear. There were a few mechanics tooling around with their maintenance droids on some of the larger commercial freighters but it looked like a slow night. It was perfect.

When we got to the Zephyr, I set my gear down and turned to Scott.

"You can change over there." I pointed to a door that led to the pilot's lounge. "Meet me back here in five. You can hang back and relax for a few minutes while inspect my vessel."

"Will do."

I walked slowly around the fuselage doing my preflight check on the atmospheric avionics and control surfaces along with the zero-grav retrojets when I saw Max working his way toward me from Dock 12. We had to go through "the ritual".

"Good evening, Nikki." Max smiled as he offered his hand after tucking his c-pad under his arm. "Looks like the Blue Zephyr Starline is about to embark on another adventure, eh?"

"How've you been, Max?" I nodded as I shook his hand. "They been keeping you busy around here?"

"It's a steady flow, and the hours are good. I'm up for a shift bid in a month."

"Moving to days?"

"Yeah, like to spend some time with the family for a change."

"Don't blame ya."

Scott had returned and nodded politely at Max as he stood quietly next to me looking casually around the hanger.

"Max, this is Fenmore Scott, a friend of mine." I smiled, "Fenny, this is Max, the shift manager."

"How do you do, sir?" Scott offered his hand.

"Pleased to meet you Mr. Scott." Max replied as they shook hands. "Okay, Nikki, let's get started, shall we?" Max grinned as he looked at his pad and took a stylus from his pocket, "Name of ship?"

"Blue Zephyr."

"Make?"

"Aerodyne 1023, Series Mx40-1A Star Chaser."

"Propulsion?"

"Primaries are Coltrane Plutonium Turbos with aftermarket Overture-12 retro-jets. Secondary sources are Watts & Rannon Magnetic Hyper-Drive Cores."

"Payload?"

"Thirty-five thousand pounds of cosmetics and luxury consumables."

"Let's go to page two," Max said unceremoniously, "Pilot name?"

"Nikki Wells."

"Age?"

"28."

"License Class?"

"Class-2 Pilot."

"Destination?"

"Cassandra City, Venus."

"Passengers?"

"One."

Max turned to Scott and pointed at him with his pen as he concentrated on the forms on his pad.

"Name of passenger?"

"Scott. First name, Fenmore."

"Passenger's age?"

"46."

"Citizenship?"

"Earth."

Max turned his attention back to me. "Purpose of journey?"

"Err, to visit friends." I said sheepishly.

"Aww common, Nikki," Max replied in an incensed tone, "'To visit friends?'"

"Why, what's wrong?"

"Ya gotta gimme something better than that. The report does get read, ya know."

"Then what do you suggest?"

"You could say something like "To visit your sick mother."."

"Okay then, "To visit my sick mother"."

"But then you better have one, and she'd better be on Venus. Then ya gotta have the proper medical forms for confirmation..."

"Look, Max," I sighed, "why are you busting my chops? Just put anything down for us that sounds good. We have to get going if we're going to make time."

"I don't even want to ask the next question about having weapons on your persons..."

"Just a Cobalt-22..."

"I'm not hearing this." Max grimaced as he rolled his eyes.

"Max we're stalling."

"Okay, okay, Nikki, don't bite my head off, I'm just..." Max trailed off and looked at the floor.

"What's the matter?"

"Nikki, don't go." Max said gravely as he looked me square in the eyes.

"What? You telling me we can't go?"

"No, I'm not saying you can't go, I'm just asking you not to."

"Max…"

"Look, we both know what you're doing and we both know where you're going, I'm just asking you not to go. Don't do it, Nikki. Walk away."

"Max, are you going to make a case out of this?"

"Yes I am." Max frowned. "I know how you're going to deviate from your flightplan. I talked to Kurlie this afternoon. Don't go Nikki."

"I have to."

"Well then don't go through the Pipe."

"I've got no choice, Max, you know that."

"You know a couple of years ago I was in your shoes…"

"Can we trade sea stories later, Max? I've got to get a move on."

"No! You're gonna listen to what I have to say, Nikki," Max snapped as he put his hand on my shoulder, "like I said, two years ago I was in your shoes. Like you I was gonna make a run. Like you I had to take the Pipe to make the time; and like you I had a bad feeling about it. I'd gone through the Pipe too many times before and I had demons nipping at my heels. I was scared. Scared of the Pipe, scared that I wouldn't come back, and scared to face guys like Kurlie. But what was I gonna do? Being a runner was all I knew how to do."

"So what am I supposed to do?"

"Walk away from it, Nikki. Don't go. You can join Patrol."

"That's absurd."

"No it's not. Isn't it better if people like us are in it? At least we understand, at least we've been there and can help out our own."

"I couldn't do that."

"Why not? The pay is good, it's clean..."

"Bribery? That's clean?"

"Well may be not." Max shrugged. "I'm only on the take as far as Departures and Flightplans are concerned, all the money in the world wouldn't get the Zephyr off the pad if I didn't think she was space-worthy. Don't go, Nikki, or you won't come back."

"What kind of thing is that to say!"

"You heard me, you will not be coming back, Nikki. I know, you will NOT be coming back."

"Is there a problem here, Nikki?" Scott asked grimly as he eyed Max.

"No. No problem, Scotty."

"Then we've better get going." Scott interrupted.

"Mr. Scott," Max turned to address my passenger to try another angle, "do you have any idea what you and Nikki are about to do during your flight?"

"No sir."

"Max, button it down." I shot him a look hoping to shut him up.

"It's insanity..." Max insisted as he shook his head. "The Pipe can be unstable at times. You could end up only God knows where if it doesn't tear you guys apart."

"Nikki, what the hell is he talking about? What is this pipe?"

"Nothing, Scotty. Nothing to worry yourself over."

"You don't know, do you Mr. Scott?" Max gasped as he shook his head unbelievingly with his eyes wide. "He doesn't know, does he, Nikki? You haven't told him. Remember what happened to Johnny?"

"That's enough Max!" I growled through clenched teeth. "That's enough!"

"He has the right to know!" Max blared.

"What's he talking about Nikki?" Scotty asked with concern as he looked at the fear in Max's eyes.

"Ignore him, Scotty, grab your things and let's go." I grimaced as I grabbed my gear. "See ya 'round, Max."

"All right," Max wilted, "You win, Nikki. I'm on the desk tonight so I'll do what I can to keep the hounds off your trail until you get to Ceres Vesta. If you make it through the Pipe in one piece stay on the sealed frequency until you get contacted by Kurlie's man. He'll give you the final coordinates to a small landing strip on the outskirts of Fluture."

We shook hands as Scott and I stepped into the Blue Zephyr. A slight chill suspend itself in the dim cargo hold of the ship as I checked to see if Kurlie's boys secured the payload properly while Scotty stuffed his bags in a stowage rack. One good thing about Kurlie's goons, they knew how to pack things tight and fasten them down thoroughly. It was makeup all right. A lot of it. About thirty containers containing powers, soaps, perfume, and lipstick; padded, packed, and stacked about twenty feet high in two rows.

powders

Kurlie even had them pack a case of hundred year old whiskey up front with a large duffle bag containing half my money along with a note:

Nikki,

No hard feelings ok cupcake? Money's all there. Half now, and the rest when you get back home. Threw in a case of my finest booze as a bonus in case you want to whet your whistle when you get to Nexus. Yes, I know, that's contraband too, but I figured you wouldn't mind this kind since it's for your personal use. Bon voyage, baby.

-Kurlie

Chapter 3

I handed Scotty a flight helmet and ushered him into the copilot's seat next to mine and began the ignition sequence. I flipped a toggle switch and the radar blipped on with its soft, lime green light and the overhead console lit up with blue, red, and yellow lights as the flight systems enabled. The bridge pressurized with a small hiss and the O2 generators began to prime the entire ship.

I set my hat on the center console as I scanned the GPS and IFA monitors and punched in my coordinates for my point of destination. I could see Max doing a final check on the pad and he waved to me as he secured the dock and closed-off launch bay access.

Five minutes later, Max sounded in on the radio "Blue Zephyr, systems check, over."

"Roger, control, Blue Zephyr confirms preflight systems run down." I replied as I adjusted the volume in my flight helmet.

"Heads-up display."

"HUD enabled."

"Avionics."

"Avionics enabled."

"Artificial gravity locks."

"AGL's check." This exchange went on for another ten minutes as we assessed communications, navigational, and cryogenic systems. Max finally gave me the green light for ignition and I dimmed the cabin lights and did one more internal payload scan within the Zephyr.

Scotty sat back and stared through the cockpit canopy at the bright overhead lights of the hanger, he was completely oblivious to the fact that he was being scanned. A small screen on my side of the instrument panel revealed the results of the sweep: all components secured, but my passenger had a porcelain sidearm in a holster strapped to his left ankle...a 9mm parabellum automatic pistol. His weight was also peculiar, he was heavier than he looked, and it just didn't add up.

The Zephyr's primary engines slowly revved-up into a high pitched whine, and I checked the fuel pressure and disengaged the heat shield as I adjusted the tint of the HUD visor that connected me to the onboard flight computer. The LED status indicated the Gamma sensors began their exterior scan and I was getting readings on ambient temperature and oxygen levels.

I flipped open the armrest on my left and inserted a DAT disc into a small computer called a Black Spyder that only I knew about. This thing was no bigger than five inches square and two inches thick, but had cost me a fortune on the black market. It was integrated into my flight computer by a Federation Techno that I had to pay on the sly to make the hook-up, but it was worth the investment.

This tiny box was a jamming device for scanners, and digital and electronic counter-measure probes. It could also intercept and scramble all transmissions the Scouts and Interceptors would use to hunt me down the moment I left our solar system. Electronically, it made me invisible.

I watched the launch bay door slowly rise in front of me and expose the darkness that encompassed the tarmac. It was a clear, windy night and the stars twinkled brightly over the city. The weather forecast in Nexus on my arrival on the 24th showed sunny skies with a 25 knot western breeze, and I looked forward to getting there and having a couple of days to myself before coming back to Earth.

"Blue Zephyr, 2-6, departure status, over." Max's voice crackled over the radio mechanically.

"Blue Zephyr, Flight 2-6, destination Venus, status green for departure, over." I replied.

"Roger, Flight 2-6. Blue Zephyr is cleared for departure on Runway-3."

The ship lurched forward and we began to roll down the runway into the night. The blue nav-lights on the sides of the airstrip twinkled and I gazed at the silhouettes of the highrises of New Detroit in the distance. I turned into the wind and idled at the end of the runway waiting for the final launch confirmation.

"Ever done space travel before, Scotty?"

"Yes."

"So hyper-speed flight is not an issue for you?"

"No issues." Scott smiled as he lowered his visor and turned his attention to the runway.

"Flight 2-6, airspace is cleared for take-off." Max crackled.

"Roger. Flight 2-6 is rolling." The engines throttled to a scream and the Zephyr vibrated slightly as I disengaged the brakes and began to accelerate down the darkened strip. I engaged the afterburners and everything around us turned into a blur as Scott and I were pushed into our seats by the g-forces as we took off.

In a matter of seconds the world below us transformed into a dark blue dome. I nosed up and entered the ionosphere. The g-suits kept our bodies stable and worked in conjunction with the Zephyr's artificial gravity locks. I took a deep breath in an effort to relax as we pushed into space at Mach 9.

As soon as we cleared the Earth's gravitational pull and crossed the Kármán line, I pulled back on a lever that extended the hypersonic drive spawnsons from the fuselage. The Zephyr trembled as the drives began to ramp-up with a drone.

I turned toward Scotty, "We're spaceborne. Let's heat it up." I smiled as I clutched the control yoke, "Going hypersonic in three...two...one, and launch." And the Zephyr shot into the blacknessof space.

I reached forward and punched my code into a number pad, and the flight computer took over. After working some calculations in my head, at the speed I planned to maintain, we may make it to the Pipe a few hours early. The very thought of traveling so fast toward something so frightening sent a chill through me, but a schedule was a schedule.

Jupiter was less than thirty minutes out and I figured we'd be outside our galaxy within the next three hours. I'd have to rely on luck when we passed the Ursa-Major system because the war had escalated with the Serenians and I hoped to dodge any cruisers from the Serenian Armada.

At our current rate of acceleration, we should max at 2.8 HsD by the time we came within range of Tal-Seti. From there we'd be a day away from the Pipe. Until then, there were always the Fed Scouts and Interceptors to dodge. I'd have my hands full if they spotted us.

No point worrying about it now. I glanced at the instrument panel and exhaled as I removed my helmet and replaced it with a wireless ocular headset. Much lighter and far more comfortable. I looked over at Scott and motioned him to remove his helmet as I handed him a spare headset.

Deep space was just a few hours out, and I had time to take a shot or two of Kurlie's parting gift. I was uptight and needed to unwind, and the thought of a stiff drink really appealed to me right now. I double-checked the auto-pilot then took off the harness and stood up to stretch my legs as Scott sat still and gazed out the canopy at the vast darkness in front of us.

I opened the bulkhead door into the cargo hold and unlatched the container with the whiskey. Perfect. I could see by the labels that Kurl spared no expense. He was a shrewd businessman, but definitely not cheap when handing out rewards. I popped open a bottle and took a long slug. I felt my stomach warm to the smoothness of the liquor and was tempted to drink some more but had to keep a clear head for the journey.

"Hey Scotty," I exhaled as I stepped up back into the bridge and held up the bottle, "care for a shot of this?"

"No thanks. I don't drink." Scott squinted and turned his head back around.

"Suit yourself." I set the bottle back in the insulated container, closed up, and backed out of the cargo bay smiling.

"Quite a view." Scotty said quietly as he peered at the points of light around us.

"Indeed. It never gets old."

Beyond the bridge's canopy lay untouchable silence. Beautiful, foreboding Space. Serenity and terror. The swirl of time and light dusted by centuries of whispers. The sheer blackness of the great beyond speckled by points of light full of worlds. For the earthbound, the distant twinkles epitomized mysteries gazed upon for generations by the light of ancient fires as elders passed lore to the young under the blanket of night. That was the same gaze that enthralled me as a child. I could lose myself in that gaze.

I looked over the monitors for any activity then reached over and turned on the Star Net-Cast receiver to catch up on daily events. Seems that the only information the news contained nowadays was all bad: the war at Bakkus coming to an end, anti-war protests on campuses throughout the galaxies, the surge of the homeless population and refugees brought on by the conflict, and the increase of crime in the outlying mining and farming colonies. It goes on and on and gets heavier by the minute.

I sighed as images blipped on the screen of a student rally being broken up by Riot Squads on Earth and Syterra-12, and was glad I took this gig. At least it got me away from the everyday troubles that faced home.

The radio chirped with an incoming transmission and I shut off the Star Net to see who was calling. It was Max. I flipped on the toggle switch and Max's voice came through the speakers.

"Nikki, you there? Nikki, you got your ears on?"

"Yes Max, I'm here."

"We're on a sealed frequency, so no one can detect this cast. How are you doing, girl?"

"So far, so good. We just pulled from our galaxy border into space about ten minutes ago so we're making good time."

"How far out 'til Event Horizon?"

"A little over a day and a half for Outer and one hour for Inner Event. Then it's just a matter of minutes."

"Nervous?"

"Yeah, I try not to think about it."

"I know."

"You know, Max, this could very well be my last run. I may retire from the game when I get back."

"I sure wish you wouldn't do this. Just circumnavigate the pipe, Nikki."

"I can't. I'll lose the rest of the pay-off and Kurlie will probably put a contract on my head for making a late drop."

"Nikki..."

"Look, the last thing I want is to have to keep looking over my shoulder for his goons to rub me out."

"I suppose you're right about Kurlie. So you're committed to seeing this through? There's no way I can talk you out of it?"

"I'll bring you back something nice from Nexus, Max."

"Listen Nikki, I've gotta sign-off. I tagged the Zephyr as a civilian subcontractor on the flight logs so you should have no problems when you get to Ceres Vesta. I'll keep an eye out for you on the screens."

"Thanks Max."

"Talk to you later."

"See ya, Max."

"So talk to me Nikki." Scott unbuckled himself from his seat, stood up, and stretched his arms as he looked over the monitors. "You and your friend Max seemed genuinely spooked by this journey we're on. What's this pipe thing Max and Kurlie were talking about?"

"Oh it's nothing to concern yourself with right now." I sighed. "I'll explain it to you when we get there."

"How about you explain it to me right now?" Scott demanded. "I think I have the right to know if we're about to do any thing out of the ordinary."

"We're already out of the ordinary, Scotty. This flight's illegal."

"Yes, I'm aware of that." Scott replied impatiently. "Talk to me."

I let out a breath and stared at the console as I shook my head.

"Well?"

"You do have a right to know. How much have you been keeping up with scientific research?"

"I haven't."

"Do you know what a wormhole is?"

"I've heard of them. Basic highschool astronomy. Pure theory."

"No, not theory, Scotty. They're out there. Closer than you imagine."

"Bullshit."

"No, it's true."

"And how do you know this?"

"Because I've been there."

"You mean you think you've seen one in real life?"

"No. I've *been* there."

"You're pulling my leg, right?"

"I'm afraid not. What Max was talking about is a conduit through space and time. We think the Pipe is a wormhole. A natural anomaly of physics--a fold in the universe. Not a lot of people believe in it for that matter. The only ones that truly believe in them are scientists; and even then, their community is split. Most theorists tend to lean more on the side of hypothesis. Makes for a nice bedtime story and spices up lectures with a wow factor."

"And you're telling me this is more than just theory. This is where we're going?"

"I'm telling you that we're not just going there, we're going into it."

"WHAT?"

"You heard me, we're going into a wormhole. The pipe. It's the only way to get to Nexus in the allotted time."

"This is a small detail that my employer seems to have neglected to tell me."

"And who would that be, Scotty?"

"Nevermind."

"You don't work for Kurlie, do you?"

"No personal questions, okay Nikki?"

"He told me you were an envoy for the product."

"I've got business at Nexus. So tell me, Nikki, has anyone else ever been through this wormhole?"

"Only three people as far as I know."

"Let me guess--you and Max..."

"Me, Max," I sighed, "and another pilot who was a close friend of ours. His name was John Tudor."

"Was?"

"It happened over a year and a half ago," I frowned, "it was Johnny's first and only time. He and Max went into the pipe during a joint run for Kurlie. They were hauling weapons and heading for the Bakkus system."

"Go on." Scotty urged quietly.

"Max told me that they just entered Event Horizon when he lost communication with John. He looked out the canopy just in time to see his ship blow apart. Totally dusted, and I mean atomized."

"Jesus."

"Not sure if you believe me, Scotty?" I smiled. "The one thing that Max's old ship had in common with the Zephyr was the magnetic hyper-drive cores. Johnny's ship, the Switchback, had nuclear powered cores. We think that may be the reason we've been able to pass through the Pipe in one piece; it may have to do with the magnetic fields generated by our ships and their reaction with the natural fields in the Pipe."

"I may have read a story or two about these, but like I've said, all theory. I've seen articles with models and illustrations of an Einstein-Rosen bridge outside our galaxy, and they were always followed by a wall of text filled with speculation, but that's it. I never paid too much attention to that science."

"Nobody ever does. Not even the military. Besides, there's always more to it than academic articles. All it takes is that one person willing to take a closer look. That one person willing to take that extra step."

"Who went in first, you or Max?"

"I did."

"How..."

"Look, it's not like I woke up one morning and decided it would be pretty cool to enter a wormhole just to see what happens." I declared impatiently. "I found it by accident. I was making a run two years ago. Hauling weapons and heading for Polaris when I was ambushed by a bandit vessel.

They cut into my frequency and threatened to blow me out of space unless I allowed them to board my ship and hijack it. This happened in the vicinity of an asteroid belt called Ceres Vesta near Tal-Seti. I changed course and ducked into the belt in an effort to lose them. I played cat and mouse with them for hours in that field until they finally scoped the Zephyr and launched a couple of anti-grav warheads.

The missiles had a target lock on me and closed-in fast. Then I saw it on my monitor. This void. For all the debris floating around in space leaving some kind of readable signature in its trek, there was something ahead of me that was clear. Something that had no trace. Turns out the Ceres Vesta asteroid belt is really an accretion disc rotating around a wormhole--a quasar, and I had gotten too close and was pulled into its jet.

The Zephyr's gravity and magnetic sensors were going crazy the whole time. Off the register. I raised the canopy's heat shield to get a visual and there it was--total blackness, and yet I was accelerating toward it incredibly fast. I was caught in the Event Horizon.

Meanwhile the sensors were going wild and the consoles were flashing red. Everything indicated missile impact on the Zephyrs fuselage but nothing happened. I should have been blown apart. Dead. Then everything stopped and went silent. Total silence. The cockpit was blacked-out and the Zephyr was drifting in darkness. The G-locks within the ship quit working and things were floating around me...pens, my ocular headset, a bottle of water.

The next thing I knew, all the lights flashed back on and I'm back in hyper-drive. The Zephyr was shaking hard, so I decelerated by ramping down the hyper-drive core. I could barely control the craft, and everything that was floating in the cockpit fell to the floor and I was pushed into my seat by the g-forces. G-forces in space, Scotty. Impossible.

I looked at the monitors and don't recognize any of the star systems around me. I started a plotter scan and started getting read-outs. I was in the Polaris region. It all happened in seconds. One second I was in Tal-Seti, the next, I'm in Polaris. It happened that fast."

"Christ." Scott gasped.

"No bandits or sign of them. No damage to the Zephyr."

"How many times have you been through this?"

"Not counting this trip, nine."

"Anything else I need to know?"

"Not really. It's just..."

"What?"

"It's just that every time I get back from a journey there's always something a little different about things. I haven't been able to put my finger on it, but things seem a tad off. People mostly."

"What do you mean?"

"Ah, nothing. May be I'm imagining it."

"No seriously, Nikki," Scott demanded, "what do you mean that people seemed off every time you come back from one of these journeys?"

"I didn't notice it right way. It took months before I began to perceive any changes in the people that I've known; there's something about the way they act or the things they do that's out of character for them."

"Maybe it's not them but you that's changed."

"Well anyway, I'll tell you one thing that changed me."

"What's that?"

"I believe in the impossible now."

Chapter 4

Kurlie

I've got less than two weeks to get a make on this guy and figure out where to go from there. Max told me Scott brought two bags with him for the trip.

"So Tommy, what did you find on this Fenmore Scott character?"

"Not much, boss. We staked him out and all we've got is that he's at the La Plume de Ma Tante Hotel. Early riser. Eats like a horse in the morning. It took a lot of digging, but we finally found out that he came from somewhere up in the northeast. Some sparrow-fart town called North River. All the data bases divulge is that he owns a couple of houses in a rural area. He seems to be a recluse.

A passenger list from the airlines show that Scott flew into New Detroit two nights ago on a red-eye and checked right into the Plume. No family, no one close to him that we can use. Records show some higher education. Spotty employment history in the trades, maybe inherited some money, but that's it."

"What else?"

"Birth records show November 3, 2360. Oregon, Earth."

"Where in Oregon?"

"I'm still looking. The trail goes cold in Oregon."

"Keep digging. This guy's got a story and I wanna know what it is. I wanna know who he works for."

"You want him taken care of when he gets to Nexus?"

"No, I want to keep an eye on him. I wanna know what kind of business he's got there. I'm gonna send Tony and Mick up north to poke around. What's that place?"

"North River."

"Get them the address to Scott's house and have them go today. Let's see what we can find out."

A couple of days passed and my boys didn't find anything up in North River except Scott's empty house being kept up by the neighbors. Nothing about this Scott's life stands out as unusual, and everything about him indicates an ordinary guy; a little too commonplace if you ask me, like he doesn't want to draw attention to himself.

His immediate neighbors don't know anything personal about him except that he's a nice landlord that brought them some firewood a couple of times. With the exception of a few small business owners that had a brief encounter with Scott, the town folk were no help either; they rarely saw him around—"Quiet fella, he seems like a nice guy...always waved and said hello when he drove by..." was the way they described him. Their opinions would be different if they had seen what he did to my men.

Then last night, Tommy came to my bar and he was scared out of his wits. He looked visibly shaken, kept looking around, and his eyes were bloodshot.

"Boss, you've gotta help me."

"You look like hell, Tommy. When's the last time you slept?"

"I haven't. I think I'm being followed."

"Calm down. Do you think anyone followed you here?"

"Maybe. I dunno."

"So what's got you so edgy?"

"This Scott guy that you've got me tracing…"

"What about him? What'd you find out?"

"I searched the C-net for anything on a Fenmore Scott; past schools, parents, siblings, military service, criminal history, you name it, and I found his personal profile. Nothing special about him, zero dirt. On the surface he seems like a citizen; pays his bills, taxes, no big deal.

He has a SCNet account like everyone else in the system, so I loaded a trackware to run a history on his SCP number so I could hack his account to see the sites he's visited along with any business transactions.

My screen went black and I couldn't get commands to work on my pad the moment I started the scan. Next thing I know, the lights in my apartment dimmed and a series of numbers started typing by themselves on the VDT.

I hit the scram switch, but my processors wouldn't turn off so I unplugged from the wall. The second I did this, my power totally blinked-out. I went out to the patio to see if may be there was a black-out in the city, but it was just my place.

I drove over to Vince's and we tried to run the scan on Scott's profile there. The same thing happened; the power went out for a few seconds and those numbers typed out on the screen again."

"So what are you getting at, Tommy?"

"Someone's watching him. I don't know who Scott is, and who ever is watching him is now watching us. Scagged our systems and did a fandango on the cores. Neither of our systems are operable."

"Can you find out who it is?"

"Vince is helping me with that right now, he's using Larron's system, but we keep hitting a firewall of some sort. We haven't been able to script it. Boss, we're up against something big here. This is some serious Network d-star system assaults."

"I thought you, Vince, and Larron were the best in the business, Tommy."

"We're good, Boss," Tommy frowned, "but I've never seen anything like this."

Tommy's sat-phone rang and he almost jumped out of his seat as he fumbled it out of his pocket. He looked at the i.d. on the screen and exhaled with a relieved expression as he looked back at me.

"It's Vince." He smiled weakly as he pressed the answer button and brought the phone up to his ear. "Vince..."

A bright flash of white light flared from the phone in Tommy's hand with a loud pop that made his head jerk violently to the side and sent him sprawling to the floor. I was sprayed instantly with his blood.

"Tommy!" I shouted as I sprang from my chair to see if he was okay. I kneeled next to his crumpled body; his face was covered with blood and the side of his head had been blown away when his phone detonated.

My bodyguards ran over, grabbed me, and pulled me away from Tommy. By then, customers began screaming as they realized that someone was killed, and pandemonium cut through the music as people jumped up and started running out of the tavern.

"Let's get'cha outta here, Kurlie!" One of them bellowed as he grabbed my arm and hustled me through the backdoors of the bar where my driver screeched my sedan to a halt in the alley.

"Tommy."

"He's dead, Kurlie!" The guard puffed as he shoved me into the backseat, slid in next to me, and nodded at my driver. "Go!"

The driver laid rubber and smoked out of the alleyway and merged into traffic into the main street.

"The safe-house on 59th and Grand." I ordered. "And wheel it!"

I exhaled and noticed my hands were trembling.

"Kurlie, you okay?" My bodyguard asked reluctantly.

"Yeah. Send some guys over to Larron's flat and get him and Vince to the safe-house. Grab all their hardware and bring it over. I want to know what they found.

Get the tavern cleaned up before the police get there. Get Tommy out of my place and get me some clean clothes."

"Sure Kurlie."

"And get Max on the line right now. I need him to contact Nikki and warn him about this guy."

I watched the traffic go by in a blur as we weaved thorough the lanes. The city went by in a strobe of distorted neon as we blazed through the sheik uptown boulevards.

My driver swerved left after passing the sonic monorail station and gunned the car through one of the busiest intersections in the city.

"Max isn't answering his telecom, Kurlie."

"Keep trying, damn it."

"We're almost there Kurlie." The driver announced with a relieved sigh as he made a right into a side street that lead to an industrial district composed of manufacturing plants and warehouses. "This place is like a ghost town after hours."

The street lights seemed dull and gave the area an ominous air as we slowly pulled up a ramp that ran along side of some loading docks of a two story building that belonged to me. We came to a stop in front of a steel roll-up door, the driver punched in a security code on a number pad, and we watched it crank up with a mechanical groan as we pulled inside a dark garage and parked.

"No Max yet?"

"No. The rest of the guys should be here soon."

"Okay, let's get set up inside and have the entire crew meet here in the next hour." I frowned as we stepped out of the car. "Somebody get the lights. I want all our safe-houses up and running within the next two hours."

"You've got it Kurlie."

"One more thing," I glared as I pulled out a cigar and lit it, "get word to all our people on the street that I want to know if there have been any big buys on weapons or drugs. I want to know if anything unusual's been going on in our territory. Nothing moves in the city without us knowing."

Chapter 5

The first four days went by without incident. I upheld my personal policy of absolutely zero transmissions and steered clear of the main shipping lanes and military supply routes. Where Scotty was concerned, we kept the small talk on neutral ground by avoiding personal questions.

In an odd way, he reminded me of my father. Wherever he originated from I could tell that he was well traveled. I still had no idea what he did for a living or what his business entailed at Nexus. Whatever it was, it couldn't be good if he was involved with Kurlie and I refused to believe that he was employed by him. No, this guy had a story. It was none of my business, but my curiosity was killing me.

The Zephyr was a light hauler but extremely maneuverable in zero grav and atmospheric environments. She had a fixed inverted gull-wing delta configuration with an eighty foot span; the vessel's double-vertical rudder's dihedral symmetry and the two smaller twenty-degree anhedral ventral fins made the craft really stable and gave me an extremely tight turning radius. The hull was a hundred and twenty feet long, thirty feet wide, and twenty-four feet tall; it was plated with poly-alloy armor composed of radar absorbing, infra-red signature reducing materials.

It cost me a fortune to get my ship customized, especially the retractable retro-jet modifications, but it was worth every credit. I took a lot of pride in black market kit bashing the instrumentation and controls to suit my needs.

The Zephyr was fast. Illegal, sensor-scrambling fast with what's called a Bokka bomb defense system that would make any smuggler drool.

The Bokka was one of a kind, it used to be the small emergency shuttle that came with the Zephyr; a Phoenix-Alpha2 parasite ship attached to the belly of the ship, but I converted it into a Bokka drone when I retro-fitted the e-pod and slide rail ejector system. It took me almost a year to get the Bokka tailored with the custom software that wasn't readily available on the black market. I had eight different techies making wafers without them knowing about each other to avoid raising suspicion, and I integrated the components myself to create the drone. The Bokka still looked like a harmless factory shuttle and could pass the scrutiny of any life-safety inspector, but it was an unlawful weapons platform armed with ion virus charges that a friend acquired for me.

The one drawback with the Zephyr was that she only had one escape pod if things went terminal. One. It was really all I needed since I traveled alone. The e-pod was sufficient to keep me alive for a while if I had to eject, but it was only designed for one person for a short duration. I've never been concerned about my escape system since I never carried passengers...until now. Let's face it, in this game every voyage had the potential of being a one way trip. It's something that I've accepted as the nature of the beast.

I looked over at Scotty and decided that he didn't have to know any more than I had already told him. He seemed more withdrawn after I disclosed our flight plan and we drew closer to the Pipe each passing day. He spent most of his time studying his SCaT Pad and basically kept to himself.

One night, as he stared blankly at the Zephyr's instrument panel (as if it could reassure him that everything would be all right), he broke his own spell with a sigh and slowly turned his head toward me and asked "So where did you learn to fly, Nikki?"

"I thought you said no personal questions." I chided playfully hoping to lighten his mood.

"Is asking how you got your pilot rating personal?"

"It is for me." I felt bad for him, he looked so dejected as he turned his attention back to the console.

"Sorry." He said weakly.

"I grew up on a farm back in the Midwest and my daddy taught me how to fly dusters when I was a teen." I smiled as I cast an eye over the plotter.

"Flying dusters and navigating a deep space freighter are two different things."

"By that you mean working on a farm knocking bugs off crops and smuggling weapons outside our solar system for a living are on opposite ends of the scale."

"Yes."

"Well to make a long story short, I was twelve the first time I made a solo flight in a duster. It was a sixty-year-old JD Fischer turbo that my father and I spent months secretly rebuilding in our barn. He'd taken me up a bunch of times in the duster that he flew, so I already knew my way around the controls. I was hooked the moment my father handed me a helmet and I strapped into the cab with him.

Anyway, it was an early spring morning, wickedly cold but the sun was out and the sky was a bright crystal blue--a perfect morning. Everyone was still sleeping when my father and I went out to the barn and hauled out the duster to a staging area at the end of the air strip. Once we got it fired-up, I hovered around next to the fields to get a feel for the controls. I'll never forget my dad's expression as he ran after me when I took off.

My spirit flew higher than the duster that morning. My mother heard the racket we were making and came out to see what the commotion was all about. She was really pissed when she saw me strafe the livestock yard and take out a section of fence before crash landing on the side of the main road. She didn't talk to my dad for a week, but I couldn't wipe the smile off of my face for a month, especially at the dinner table when my dad would wink at me when mom and my brothers weren't looking.

Years later when my father died, I felt like I had nowhere else to go. My mother and brothers inherited the farm, and we all got a percentage of the property rights. Then there was an insurance pay-out from daddy's death. My father

70

stipulated in his policy that eighty percent was to be given to me when I turned seventeen. I couldn't see myself living there the rest of my life, so I turned my property share over to Mom, then took my cut from the policy, moved to New Detroit, and forged my own business after working for the Aerodyne/Genesis Corporation for a year.

You know, growing up, my father used to tell me there where worlds out there I needed to see...he told me to "dream beyond the fields and fences." When he was home, we used to sit in the backyard with the telescan and look at the star systems on clear nights and chart them.

"What did you mean when you said "when he was home"? Was your father gone a lot?"

"Yes, he was gone for long periods of time. My mother and brothers were the ones that really kept the farm running."

"You and your father sounded close."

"Yeah, we were tight. I was his only daughter and the youngest in the family, so that kind of made me.."

"A daddy's girl." Scott grinned. "I've been meaning to tell you that I thought the way you handled that lizard at Montrell's bar the other night was impressive."

"You saw that, did you?" I grinned as I shook my head.

"Where did you learn to fight like that?"

"When you grow up with three older brothers you sort of have to be able to stand up for yourself."

"You really expect me to believe that you're self-taught with those kind of moves?"

"You really expect me to believe that you're going to Nexus on business involving cosmetics?" I squinted as I took a closer look at the scanner. "And what's up with your personal weight, Scotty? When you boarded my ship you tipped in at a hefty two hundred seventy-three pounds, someone with your build should be at one eighty. There something you need to tell me?"

"Wouldn't know where to start, Nikki."

"How 'bout with something simple, like an explanation about your weight. Tell me that and I'll ignore the fact that you've got a 9-mill strapped to your left ankle."

"Okay," Scotty nodded his head with a resigned grin, "I've got artificials."

"How much of you?"

"Legs and my left arm are integrated bio-mech."

"May I?" I reached over and pulled up Scotty's left sleeve and ran my hand over his left forearm. "Your peripherals look and feel real," I gasped, "your arm feels natural...a warmth, I've never seen anything like it. They did a nice job on you. Can you feel me touching your arm?"

"Yes, I can feel your touch. Cutting edge technology."

"What happened to your real limbs?"

"Car accident."

"You're lying. This kind of technology isn't available to the general public yet, even the best AI's don't have this kind of finish. You're artificials are flawless. So what happened to your real ones?"

"I'll keep it simple, young lady. I lost my legs and arm during the Terekian war. I don't remember much. All I have are fragments that I'm still trying to piece together."

"You had to have been someone important to get implants like those. The Council put serious money into you."

"So where did you learn to ~~fly?~~" FIGHT

"My father."

"You're not going to tell me your father was a farmer versed in close quarter combat, are you?"

"Yes I am." I exhaled sadly as I turned to look at the instrument panels. "Looks like we both lost something to the war. You lost your limbs, and I lost my father. He was a pilot with Fleet."

"Okay, Nikki." Scotty nodded. "Are you satisfied with my answers?"

"Not really, but it'll have do for now."

"Truthfully, the less you know about me the better off you'll be in the long run."

"Funny, I was just thinking the same thing for you and our flight through the Pipe."

Charon. I had him memorized. I knew his face, I knew his habits, I knew where he liked to go on certain days and the times he went there. I knew his life. I just about had the lay-out of Fluture mapped in my head and began visualizing the logistics of how I was going to get myself in range undetected, make my move, and get out.

Charon had two places he liked to call home: a sixteenth floor penthouse in the La Rouge Hotel of the casino that he ran in the heart of Fluture, and his two story villa located among vineyards on the side of the Sertina's Pass mountain range overlooking the city. I decided Charon's life would end at his villa.

Before I left North River I sent in a laundry list of items I wanted for the mission. Drop spots should have been arranged for me by now, all I had to do was get there, pick up what I wanted, and set up the hit. I would be alone for that part. Everything would be on me. If I was successful, the pay-off would be tremendous. If I failed and got caught, I'd die as an unknown. I had my fingertips sanded before I left home and did a chemical scrub on my body known as "scaling". Now I'm untraceable. I am become invisible.

If something happened to me, officials would be working for a long time trying to find out who I was and where I came from.

Nikki asked a few probing questions but it was no big deal. I learned more about her than she did about me. She had a slight accent that was barely detectable, and she always seemed to be on edge. I had to be careful with her, she seemed to have a talent for reading people, and an eye for detail.

I sensed that Nikki wasn't telling me everything about our voyage and that was fine. I figured if I didn't ask her too many questions she would reciprocate by withholding her own queries.

Chapter 6

"Nikki, do you copy?" It was Max, and from the tone of his voice, this sounded urgent. "Nikki can you hear me?"

"Yes Max, what's going on?" I pressed my left hand over the ear piece of my headset and leaned forward. Scotty had sunk into his seat and fallen asleep.

"I've got a signature on my screen showing that you've got company out there."

"Details?"

"None yet. You're so far out it could be anyone."

"Nothing on my side yet. How far way are they from me?"

"Two hundred miles. One craft. It's about the size of a Class-3 freighter..."

"Okay, I've got 'em, Max, they just blipped on the scanner." A transmission chimed-in on my headset. I could see on the panel it was coming from the ship--a looped message on the general call network.

"...CQD, this is the Moria Balá...need assistance...CDQ, this is the Moria Balá..."

"Max, I've got an incoming communication on another push. Looks like a distress call."

"Be careful, Nikki. Could be a siren."

"Thanks for the heads-up, Max." I disengaged the auto-pilot, took control of the Zephyr, and steered in the direction of the distress call.

"Trouble Nikki?" Scotty asked quietly as he yawned and stretched.

"We're not alone."

"What's up?"

"Not sure yet, but it looks like a disabled ship."

"Anything I can do?"

"Yeah, relax and let me do my job." I said firmly as I double checked the Black Spyder and slowed down to a sub-hypersonic speed and put the drives on coast.

"...CQD, this is the Moria Balá...need assistance...CDQ, this is the Moria Balá..."

I didn't have it in me to ignore the call, and if this was a ship in trouble I couldn't live with myself if I abandoned other humans in space. So for the first time in my career, I broke the first rule of smuggling and keyed my headset.

"Mark One, Moria Balá, come back."

"CQD, this is the Moria...this is Captain Seinz of the Moria Balá, can you hear me? Over."

"Roger Moria Balá," I responded calmly, "your transmission is clear."

"Please identify. Over."

"This is the pilot of the Blue Zephyr, Captain Seinz. What's your status? Over."

"Blue Zephyr, we were attacked by a bandit vessel. My ship is disabled and I have wounded on board. We've been adrift for two days. Can you assist?"

"I've marked your position, Captain. I'll send a call out for an SAR team to come for you when we get close enough to the main shipping lanes."

"Blue Zephyr, my wounded are critical, I need to get them off board and get them the proper medical attention . Can you dock?"

I turned to Scotty and shook my head. "I've got a bad feeling about this."

We were about to make a pass less than six kilometers away from the Moria Balá. We would still be a fairly safe distance from them and out of visual range.

"I'm going to run a probe on them."

The flight computer profiled the craft and the image showed up as a 3D model on one of the video display units.

"You don't trust the captain, Nikki?"

"No way. Even if they've been drifting for two days how the hell did they get way out here? We're too far from the lanes for them to have floated this far off course."

Suddenly, the cabin filled with a bright flicker of orange light followed by the sound of thunder as a warhead detonated a thousand meters in front of us. The Zephyr shuddered and the cabin lights blinked on and off as we were jostled hard against our seats. We could hear the clatter of debris slamming against the fuselage as we flew through the shrapnel.

"Damn it!" I shouted angrily as I clutched the yoke and stabilized the Zephyr.

"Are we hit?"

"I don't see any breach in our hull!" I glowered as I looked at the diagnostic panel for red blinking lights. "That was close!"

Another transmission from the Moria piped over the cast, "Blue Zephyr, power down and surrender your ship or we will fire on you again!"

"I knew it!" The probe showed that the Moria had fired-up its engines and began to turn in our direction. "Hang on, it's time to turn-n-burn. I'm going to try to out run them!"

"Blue Zephyr, you cannot escape. Power down and prepare to be boarded."

Getting hijacked is one thing, but what the pirates would do to a female if they captured me was another. "Captain Seinz, why don't you pack five pounds of sodium azide in the crack of your ass and get blistered!" I growled as I punched an overdrive button and launched us into spontaneous hypersonic flight.

"You just signed your own death warrant, pilot!" Seinz snarled. "I'm going to skin you alive and roll you in salt. Before I'm done, you will be begging me to put an end to your pitiful life!"

"That ship's fast!" I hissed as I looked at the vector scanner to get a fix on their position. "They just went hypersonic."

"Don't you have any weapons systems to protect yourself?"

"We're a civilian freighter," I was about to tell Scotty about the Bokka but decided against it for now, "we have to rely on Fleet or ISP officers to defend us from parasites like Seinz."

"And we're an illegal flight so..."

"...so we're as lawless as they are and basically shit out of luck."

We almost had a hundred and fifty mile lead, but the Moria was closing on us fast. I accelerated and hoped we could put enough distance between us to discourage a pursuit. If I extended the sonic drive shrouds to shield the magnetic trace from the spawnsons, they would smother the magnetic fields the drives needed to maximize our speed. I kept the canopy's particle heat shield up so I could actually see what was in front of us as we blazed through the chill of deep space.

"We're still two days out from Tal-Seti, but we can definitely shake them off our ass if we can reach the Ceres Vesta belt."

"Okay, do what you have to do." Scotty replied through clenched teeth.

"I was figuring on maxing 2.8 HsD but we're going to have to push the drives harder. You'd better tighten your harness, Scotty, I'm going to burn the pipe and try to knock a few more hours off our flight time."

"How fast can your ship go?"

"I can get 4.5 HsD, but the Zephyr can't maintain that speed for too long or the cryogen squelch piping will rupture and we'll burn-out the inter-coolers."

"Then what happens?"

"Then we're a dead stick. We may as well initiate the self-destruct sequence and vaporize ourselves before Seinz gets to us."

"I don't think we've got much of a choice, Nikki. You're going to have to push the Zephyr."

"He's pissed." I snickered softly as I bit my lower lip and gave Scotty an embarrassed look.

"You think? You told him to pack his ass." Scotty smiled.

"He fired on us then threatened to skin me alive! Not exactly the kind of thing a girl likes to hear during the holidays."

"Do you always get in this much trouble, Nikki?"

"Not if I can help it."

"I mean first it was that guy at Kurlie's bar, now you've got this Seinz in love with you..."

"Okay, so I'm having a bad week," I feigned angrily as I tried to keep a straight face, "you may want to tread lightly, Scotty, I'm not above lobbing an insult your direction to keep you in your place."

"You're all heart." Scotty smiled widely as he turned his attention back to the view outside the canopy.

"We're at 3.2 now. I'm hoping Seinz isn't going to be able to keep up with us ."

"What if he can?"

"He needs to be able to see us first. Any vector scan or IMF probe he does will be a waste of time, we're shielded electronically. If he tries to get a thermal image on our heat signature he'll be out of luck. We're purely hypersonic--have been since I shut down the thrusters when we cleared Earth's gravitational pull, so he can't track us by infra-red. We also don't leave any ion or radiation trails because the Zephyr has magnetic drives. The only two ways Seinz could track us is if the Moria can zero-in on our drive's magnetic emissions or he actually gets a visual on us."

"How visible is our magnetic trail?"

"There are a lot of things floating around out there that have magnetic fields--meteorites, asteroids, charged particles in the solar winds, not to mention plasma streams and transient energies. Seinz would have to ferret the Zephyr's profile out of that fodder and get within a hundred mile radius to get an accurate reading on our course, but then again..."

"But then again—what?"

I sighed. "I've seen a lot of things since I've been in the business. Black market techies are willing to make just about anything if you've got the cash or credit to pay them off...no questions asked propositions. God only knows what kind of systems the Moria has onboard and where he got them." I shook my head with disdain and exhaled. "I farking hate pirates."

"Is there a difference between bandits and pirates?"

"Bandits steal. Pirates kill."

I held our trajectory steady and kept an eye on the scanner for the Moria Balá as we pushed into the infinite sub-zero blackness toward the Pipe. Thousands of light years ahead, the vast blue and orange beauty of the Lucky CN 1051 Nebula filled the cockpit canopy. The central star pulsed with a rhythm as if the birth of another solar system was being announced to the rest of the universe.

"Tell me about Nexus. Kurlie said you knew the planet like the back of your hand."

"What do you want to know? Demographics?"

"I was thinking along the lines of night life. You know, dance clubs, parties, shows..."

"Nikki, do I look like the type of guy that goes to dance clubs?"

"You never know about a person, you don't exactly fit the profile of anyone that would do business with Kurlie, either."

"I think you'll love it there. The days are thirty-six hours long, so you'll have plenty of time to recover from any of the festivities you plan to attend."

"Once this drop is made, I'll refuel and tune-up the Zephyr for the trip back, it usually takes about two days depending on how much particle damage there is on the hull."

"Are you going to need help with that?"

"Nah, it's not that big a deal most of the time, and I can usually hire a mechanic for the heavier work if one of the larger panels needs to be replaced."

"Let me know if you want to share the repair costs."

"Thanks, Scotty." I smiled warmly as I glanced at him. I was really starting to like this guy. "When I'm done, I'd like to hang back for a few days to rest before we start back to Earth. You know, poke around Nexus and get a feel for the culture."

"When do you want to leave?"

"We arrive in Fluture on Tuesday morning at 0530. Meet me back at the Inter-port on Sunday the 29th at the same time, I want to get an early start home. Will that give you enough time to take care of your business?"

"Perfect, you've got a deal."

"Get some rest, Scotty."

"What about you?"

"I've got a ship to fly. No sleep for the wicked."

The hours stretched out in ragged strands coiled with apprehension. I was worried about Seinz, I've encountered hijackers before, but they've never been able to put the fear

85

in me like this guy--even without knowing what he looked like, he frightened me. Yes, his threats were barbaric and unsettling, but it wasn't limited to what he said, it was in how he said it. Call it a woman's intuition, but there was just something in his voice that set my internal alarm off and terrified me. It seemed to change the energy that surrounded us--it was dark, soulless, and reptilian. I had a feeling that vaporizing me wouldn't satisfy Seinz. No, he struck me as a sadist that wanted more from his victims. He wants to see them suffer, writhe, and beg.

Another cause for concern was the Moria's speed, she looked like a formidable ship, and I've never seen a vessel that size move so fast; and last but not least, the missile he fired at us; judging from the burst, it had to be a military grade warhead. God only knows how and where he got ordnance like that and what else he had in his arsenal.

I edged the Zephyr closer to her maximum speed and held her there for a couple of hours then backed-off the drives before they squelched. I rubbed my eyes and yawned. I couldn't remember ever being so tired on any journey.

As we neared the Ceres Vesta asteroid belt, the instrument panel twittered three times. "Damn!" I cussed raptly as I shot a look at the vector scanner.

"What's wrong?" Scotty snapped awake and clutched the armrests of his chair.

"As if we didn't have enough problems," I pointed at the monitor, "see those four red dots blipping ahead of us?"

"What are they?"

"I can't tell yet, give the scanner a minute to get us a profile. They may be harmless navigation buoys based on their spacing. They're just in our path for now."

I exhaled as the computer began constructing a model of the crafts ahead, then turned my attention on tracker to see where the Moria was positioned.

"Eighty miles and closing." I clenched my teeth hard and frowned. "Seinz is on our trajectory."

"Nikki, what the hell are those things in front of us?" Scotty scowled as he stared at the monitor at the rotating 3D images. The VDU revealed four unmanned crafts, each with armored dome fuselages twenty feet in diameter and six segmented tentacles trailing forty feet behind them.

"Oh that's just great, Serenian terminus drones. Seekers."

"How far are they?"

"Hundred and twenty miles out, but I'm going to draw them in."

"WHAT?"

"You heard me. Look, Seinz is gaining on us and we're less than two hours away from Ceres Vesta. I don't think we're going to be able to outrun him." I pointed at the vector scanner and the VDU. "I've got a plan, we get those Seekers and the Moria to zero-in on us, if I time it right, maybe we can get the drones to go after Seinz's ship and we can slip through."

"Risky." Scott sighed as he rubbed his brow.

"It's our only chance. We need to disable the Moria or we'll never make it to the Pipe."

"Okay, Nikki, I trust your judgment."

"One more thing, Scotty."

"What's that?"

"Seinz doesn't know you're here, as far as he's concerned, I'm the only one on board. If this doesn't work and he boards us," I looked over at Scotty grimly, "there's an epod in the cargo hold, I want you to get in and eject. I'll keep them distracted while you get away. The auto-pilot is enabled by default and should get you to the lanes. You should get picked up by a freighter."

"And what are you going to do?"

"I've got the shuttle," I lied, "I'll get out when I get the chance."

"If not?"

"Captain goes down with the ship. It's an old, unspoken code of honor. Once Seinz is on board I'll blow-up the Zephyr and take him with me into the afterlife in a blaze of glory."

"Nikki..."

"It's not as bad as it sounds, one thing that will come out of this is that smugglers will be telling this story for years to come." I smiled.

"You're crazed."

"Hang on to your ass!" I bellowed as I flipped on the toggle switches and fired the thrusters. The Zephyr punched forward with the added power surge as the rockets flared to life and gave the ship a bright heat signature as we hit 4.8 HsD.

"It's working, the Seekers are moving toward us!" I laughed maniacally as I looked at the VDU. "Damn! We're hauling ass!" I hooted as I checked our speed.

"Zephyr," Seinz's voice boomed over the intercom, "ramp down and surrender!"

"Eat carbon, you asshat!" I spit back into the intercom knowing he could track us by infra-red now.

The Moria was less than twenty miles away when they fired several missiles. The first one detonated three hundred feet in front of us, and large superheated shrapnel smashed into our fuselage as we hurled through the daggers of particle lite and fire...

"Goddamn it!" I screamed as I banked a hard left and nosed down thirty-five degrees in an evasive maneuver; that pitched the gyroscope wildly in the opposite direction and the drives screamed...

...the second warhead exploded less than a hundred feet on our left and almost threw us into a spin. The heat from the blast scathed the hull and shredded a main RAM panel. Scotty was jolted hard in his seat and I could barely hear him cussing as the detonation engulfed us with a thunderous boom and bright flash of light...

...the Zephyr rocked sideways and the instrument panels and overhead console lit-up in red as alarms sounded...the third missile blew up and ripped a portion of the left vertical rudder to pieces and punctured one of the main cryogen pipes feeding the right hypersonic drive...

I throttled the drives back and ramped down to exit hypersonic. I kept the thrusters on and drove forward as the whine of the drives began to recede. I could see the image of the Moria Balá on the VDU...they had caught up to us and matched our speed.

Seinz brought the ship two hundred feet above the Zephyr. It was a lot larger than I thought; the Moria was a dark, steely grey with reactive armor and a series of probes grouped at the front of her hull. From what I could see up close, the craft was at least three times larger than the Zephyr and looked like a Serenian deep space battle cruiser.

I looked at Scotty and nodded, "Get to the pod." I said calmly as I looked at the vector scanner. "When you see the door of the decon chamber open, eject."

Scotty stood up steadily, grabbed his flight helmet, and walked to the bulkhead door to the pressure-lock that led back to the hold.

"Good luck, Nikki." He said sullenly, then stepped into the lock.

The thrusters of the Moria Balá burned radiantly in the blue-black void of space, and I could see their flicker reflected off the surface of the cockpit anti-glare panel. I looked up through the glass canopy and saw the retro-jets on the bottom of the Moria's massive hull firing in an even pattern to slow down as they loomed over us. I also noticed a ball gun turret with the twin barrels of a pulse cannon trained at my cockpit. We were at cruising speed but the chase was over.

I sighed and I punched in my code to initiate the self-destruct sequence and set it for a silent countdown. All that was left was the voice command...

Chapter 7

I flipped the drives to idle and they slipped into a quiet hum that was ghosted by the drone of the thrusters. The Zephyr was damaged and wouldn't be able to take a pounding like that again.

"Cut your main burners, pilot." Seinz's voice ordered coldly through the cast.

I reached forward and hit the toggles and the jets began to shut down.

"Aviator, engage your auto-pilot and maintain cruising speed. Keep the gravity cells enabled and prepare to be boarded." Another male voice commanded on my headset.

The seconds ticked by painfully slow. I took a deep breath and cringed at the thought of what lay in store for me in the time I had left. Scotty should be ejecting soon. I hoped he would be able to get safely to the shipping lanes.

The Zephyr's cargo bay had a simple lay-out; there was a small overhead crane on a track running above a narrow center aisle. The floor was a grated poly-alloy that allowed for the cross-ventilation of cargo. The containers of cosmetics were stacked on each side of the aisle in two rows twenty feet high from front to back for fast, easy unloading.

A minute later a small shuttle had deployed from the Moria and descended to the right side of the Zephyr where the docking port was located. There was a heavy clang as it clamped to the port collar and the decon chamber in my ship began to depressurize.

The stainless steel locking bolts of the port hatch beeped electronically and opened with a mechanical whirr. The neoprene seals hissed softly and the thick hatch swung open as light from the foreign ship flooded the chamber. A faint whine of fans penetrated the silence as a small airborne reconnaissance drone hovered into the compartment and paused to survey the area.

The sensor for the bulkhead door to the cargo hold chirped twice, a LED status light mounted above the entrance blinked green, and the door automatically slid open. The probe hung in the chill for a few seconds, then crossed the threshold. The Zephyr was officially invaded.

The automaton floated six feet above the floor and drifted slowly into the Zephyr's dark hold between the crates. Suddenly, the drone projected a thin, pale blue light and began to scan the cargo hold from the grated floor to the perforated ceiling panels as it glided forward in the direction of the cockpit.

Seconds later, shadows emerged through the door of the chamber and the gloom was pierced by thin red beams from the laser sights of assault rifles. Three figures appeared and slowly moved forward through the dim compartment single file.

Scott stretched out on top of a group of crates located in the middle of the cargo hold. He inched forward to the edge of the container and peered down as the probe hovered past him. He controlled his breathing and closed his eyes as he reached down and pulled a Black Raven automatic pistol from a nylon holster strapped to his leg.

He watched in silence as he sized-up the bandits when they passed below him. Scott could tell from their silhouettes that two of them were wearing night vision goggles, but all of them were trussed in ballistic vests. He could also see the plumes of breath being expended from their rebreathers. The pirates knew how to move through unfamiliar space to an extent, but they weren't professional soldiers. They were careful in the way they pressed through the cargo bay--they kept their spacing eight feet apart and two constantly scanned the opposite areas to their sides while the pointman focused on what was in front of them. Their only mistake was a fatal one: they neglected their overhead and relied too much on the reconnaissance drone for accurate information. Amateurs.

Scott attached the flash and sound suppressor to the pistol and flicked off the safety. As far as he was concerned, they walked right into a kill zone...

I heard the bulkhead door to the pressure lock slide open, a few seconds passed then the cockpit door opened and a probe trekked into the bridge and came to a hover less than a foot away from my face. I felt the small wafts of air from its power source buffeting gently against my skin and could hear the whirr of small servos as it adjusted its pitch to maintain level flight in front of me.

"Aviator," a deep, electronically enhanced voice sounded from behind, "remain facing forward, put your hands on your head, and stand."

I raised my arms slowly and laced my fingers together as I placed them on top of my head. The probe stayed at eye level as I rose to my feet. Why hasn't Scotty ejected yet? Why is he still on board? I wondered as I stared out the canopy.

The intruders stood in a half circle around me with their weapons raised. "Pilot, turn and face me." The one behind me ordered.

They removed their rebreathers and I was surprised to see the one to my right was a female. She was a little taller than I was and had straight, platinum blond hair that fell to her shoulders. Her emerald-green eyes were cold and unnerving; I could see her lean frame even with a kevlar vest and rebreather pack on.

The two men were a little over six feet tall. The tallest of the trio was also the oldest--probably in his mid-forties. He was also the one that gave the orders. His skin was fair, and he had red hair pulled back into a ponytail. He frowned as he eyed me suspiciously. The second male had short, dark hair; and there was a nasty scar that ran from his left temple down to his chin.

"So you're the one that interrupted my dinner and pissed-off Seinz." The younger male said menacingly as he passed his eyes over me. "You're just his type," he grinned as he eased his weapon down and took a step closer, "mine too."

"Keep it tucked, Edik." The female interjected. "No one touches her for now."

"Oh come on, Echo," the young male replied as he frowned at his female shipmate, "just let me have a little fun with her. Seinz don't have to know."

"In your dreams, numbnuts." I growled. "Not in this lifetime or the next."

"Woo! I'm gonna have to teach you some manners." Edik snarled as he leaned into my face.

I could feel his breath as he brought his head down and sniffed the left side of my neck behind my ear. I turned my head the other way and closed my eyes in disgust. "EEW!"

"Edik that's enough!" Echo said firmly. "You'll have plenty of time to use her later."

"Mmmm!" Edik exhaled loudly as he closed his eyes. "You smell delicious..." he smacked.

"And you...just smell." I grimaced. "You remind me of something I saw floating in the water closet of a public restroom, except the lump of shit had more personality than you." I smiled.

"Why you little…"

"Give it a rest, Edik." Echo smirked as she put her hand on his shoulder and pulled him back. She kept her weapon pointed at me. "What was your point of origin, pilot?"

"Earth."

"What was your destination?"

"Medusa."

"Solo flight, thousands of miles away from the main shipping lanes, and we didn't detect any distress signals from you when we fired on your vessel." Echo stated matter-of-factly. "You're a smuggler."

"That means she has no manifest." Edik leered.

Echo shouldered her rifle and turned to Edik, "Cover me. I'm going to pat her down for weapons."

She took a step closer and gestured for me to turn around. "Take off the jacket slowly."

I removed my bomber jacket, let it fall to the floor, and put my hands back on my head.

"Look what we've got here," Echo smiled as she grabbed my Cobalt from the shoulder holster, and handed it to Edik.

"What do you have in the hold?" The older man demanded.

"Deodorants and skin care products for androgynous, ponytailed male hijackers."

"Wiseass!" He pressed the barrel of his rifle between my eyes. "I otta blow your fu..."

"Back off Grey." Echo said calmly as she took my tactical knife from its sheath. "Seinz wants her alive for now." She continued to pat me down. Echo paused for a second and sighed as she removed the ankle wrap with the spikes and tossed it to Edik. "Why don't you make yourself useful and see what she's got in the back?"

Edik examined the spikes and shook his head.

"Yeah, Edik, take the probe and check it out." Grey ordered. "Echo, can you run a diagnostic on this ship?"

"I'll work on access." Echo said sternly as she stood back up and stared at me. "She's clean." Echo nodded then backhanded my left cheek hard. "You'll do what you're told if you know what's good for you."

"Grey what's your status?" A deep voice sounded over the older man's headset.

"The ship's secure, Seinz. It's just the pilot--no passengers."

"Send someone back to the shuttle and find out what's going on with Rell." Seinz said angrily. "I've been trying to reach him for the last ten minutes. If he's asleep at the controls again I'm going to dump his ass out here."

"Give us a few more minutes and I'll have Edik look in on him."

"What's she hauling?"

"Don't know yet. Edik's checking on the cargo now."

"Hurry it up. We just picked something up on the scanners. Something's heading toward us."

"10-4, Seinz." Grey said humorlessly. He put his hand over the left ear piece of his headset. "Rell, you copy?"

Silence.

"Rell, you there?" Grey shook his head with disgust. "Bastard!"

"Seinz is right," Echo glanced over from the instrument panel, "he probably fell asleep again. You know how he is."

A few minutes later, Edik reappeared with a bottle and the duffle bag.

"What's that?" Grey asked.

"First crate I opened is full of this hooch!" Edik beamed as he took a swig of whiskey and belched."

"Gimme that!" Grey snagged the bottle out of Edik's hands and studied it. "Moving alcohol across space." Grey raised the bottle to his nose and sniffed. "This is the good stuff."

"Alcohaulin'!" Edik grinned. "And check this out!" He held up the bag.

"What's in it?"

Edik set the duffle bag on the floor, unzipped it, and stood back up with a huge smile.

"Damn!" Grey's eyes widened as he stared at my money. "Anything else we should know about?" Grey frowned.

"Yes, the dietary supplements I've been taking give me a nasty case of the vapors, how does my ass smell?"

"This one's trouble, Grey," Edik glared as he held up my ankle wrap, "I say you let me have at her for a few, then we end her and tell Seinz she tried to pull some shit."

"Shut up, Edik!" Grey spat. "Get back to the shuttle and wake up Rell. We're bringing her back to the Moria."

Edik shouldered his rifle and stomped through the pressure lock. The drone followed him through as the door slid shut and he headed back to their ship...

Scott moved silently into the shadows of the last stack of containers that stood next to the door of the decon compartment when he heard footsteps coming down the aisle. He stood motionless in the darkness with his back against the wall and his weapon in his left hand.

The pirates had gotten careless and assumed Nikki was alone. This was a mistake Scott would exploit. He let Edik walk by and enter the chamber.

"Rell, you dumbass!" Edik bellowed as he stepped into the shuttle and trudged into the cockpit where he saw his partner sitting in the pilot seat facing forward. "Wake up you idiot! Grey's really pissed!" He grabbed Rell's right shoulder and shook him.

Rell's head lolled back and forth lifelessly and his body slumped forward and fell against the instrument panel. Edik jumped back in shock and turned around when Scott pulled the trigger of the Raven and put two rounds into Edik's forehead. The back of Edik's skull blew open and canopy was splattered with blood, small lumps of gray matter, and bone as his body was thrown backwards from the impact.

Scott grabbed the drone and smashed it against the wall where it blew apart with a shower of sparks and smoke. He moved quickly through the Zephyr's cargo hold with the Raven drawn in front of him and stopped at the bulkhead that led to the cockpit...

The Zephyr shook hard and almost knocked me off balance when warheads detonated and rocked the Moria Balá. I looked through the canopy and saw the flash of the Moria's pulse cannons firing rapidly; the Seekers had arrived and were making their run. They homed-in on Seinz's heat signature and strafed his vessel with their pulse cannons.

"We need to get back to the ship!" Grey shouted as he turned his attention to the unfolding chaos outside.

I started laughing when one of the Serrenian drones attached itself to the Moria's fuselage and drove a tentacle through a gun turret and began pulling the panels apart.

"Echo! Let's get back to the shuttle!" Grey shouted in a panic as he stumbled backwards toward the pressure lock. "Let's go! Let's go!"

Echo grabbed her rifle and growled. "What about her?"

Grey looked at me. "What the hell are you laughing at?"

"Sequence, 3M-TA3." I chortled, "Initiate."

"What the hell was that?" Echo blurted.

The bridge lights dimmed, flickered brightly three times, and began to pulse in red. "The beginning of the end." I smiled and glanced at the control panel. "Seinz can you hear me?"

"Who is this?" Seinz screamed back over the intercom. I could hear the pandemonium of his crew's hysterical shouts mixed with loud popping noises and explosions in the background as the Moria engaged the Seekers in battle.

"How do you like our new friends?"

"I think she enabled the ship to self-destruct!" Echo piped as she looked at the blinking lights on the instrument panels.

"YOU DID THIS!" Seinz roared.

"Hubba-hubba-hubba!" I laughed.

Grey stepped into the pressure lock and the door to the cargo hold slid open. "Echo, NOW!" He yelled and turned, "Let's get the hell out of..." Scott stepped in front of him and punched his throat with a left jab before he had a chance to finish his sentence. Grey's eyes widened with surprise as he dropped his weapon and clutched his neck; he made a loud croaking noise then his eyes rolled white before he collapsed into a crumpled heap on the floor.

"Grey!" Echo screamed in horror as she turned her attention to her fallen comrade. I dropped to the floor and spun counter-clockwise with a leg sweep that knocked Echo off her feet and sent her sprawling on her back against the grating while her rifle bounced out of her hands and landed a few feet away.

Echo jumped back up immediately and pulled out a Kirsten Automatic pistol as I dove for her assault rifle, grabbed it, and fired a burst into her abdomen as I lay prone on the floor. The impact slammed her against a support column, and her body went limp as she slid down to her knees and fell face first to the grating.

"Bitch!" I cussed.

"Nikki, you okay?" Scotty asked.

"We need to get these scumbags off the Zephyr and strap in!" I replied as I picked up Echo's sidearm.

The Zephyr lurched hard to the right and we were thrown against a bulkhead. I staggered awkwardly to my seat and squinted through the canopy at the flickering particle lites from the laser fire outside. A Seeker ripped a huge panel from the Moira's fuselage and penetrated her hull...

"Scotty!" I shouted hoarsely. "We need to jettison that goddamn shuttle that's attached to us or we're screwed!"

...a blinding bluish-white light flashed from the Moria--it seemed to pull everything into a vacuum of silence that lasted forever...I held my hands up to shield my eyes and time lapsed into a slow motion drift as jagged shadows danced on the bridge...

...a fraction of a second, and an internal explosion from the Moria blew out a section of her hull with an orange ball of flame. Something had ignited their O_2 generators and she was actually on fire...

...a secondary blast sent fragments spinning through the darkness and debris clattered loudly against the Zephyr...I looked up and the severed upper body of one of the pirates drifted by the canopy...

"Oh god!" I cried as I put a hand over my mouth and turned away.

"Nikki!" Scotty yelled through the mayhem, "What do we need to do?"

I regained my composure and leaned over the flight panel. "Terminate false load exercise, password: Faraday."

The cabin lights stopped blinking and I double-checked the auto pilot. The drives were still on cruising speed and I could see the Moria Balá slowly pulling away from us with her guns blazing.

"Let's get these two back to their ship and ditch'em!"

Scotty frisked Grey's wilted body and fished out my Cobalt. "Nikki, your heater."

"Thanks." I grinned as I holstered my weapon.

He grabbed Grey roughly and slung him effortlessly over his left shoulder. I flipped Echo over with the intent of dragging her by her arms when I saw where I had shot her. "Gee-zus!"

"What's wrong?" Scotty asked as he carried Grey over to where I was standing.

"She's a friggin' AI!" I exclaimed as I stared at the exposed wires still sparking and sticking out of her stomach. Echo's eyes were still open but the cornea of her left eye was glass black.

"I'll be damned." Scotty scoffed. "Come on, we'd better hurry!"

The Zephyr pitched sideways and shook hard as we moved Grey and Echo's bodies through the cargo hold, pushed them back into their shuttle, and closed their access door. I slammed the port hatch and engaged the locks as Scotty and I backed out into the decon chamber.

"We're done. Let's get back to the bridge!" I exhaled.

We strapped ourselves into our seats as I watched the Moria tangle with the Seekers. Two of them had already attached themselves to their ship and were pulling it apart. Even with the distance between us, we could hear the "Thunks!" of armor-piercing rounds boring through the Moria's hull as the other battle drones fired their cannons with every high speed pass.

I leaned forward and slammed my hand on a button that detonated a ceramic ring around the docking port. The Zephyr trembled as the shuttle blew free and floated lifelessly into the void.

"Hang on, Scotty!" I grabbed the control yoke, pulled back, and banked left as a Seeker took a direct hit from one of the Moria's pulse cannons, spun wildly by us, and smashed into the shuttle at full speed. We were pushed against our seats as they exploded and the bridge rattled from the blastwave.

"Son-of-a-bitch that was close!" Scotty shouted over the din.

"Powering up!"

"Let's go! Let's go!" Scotty drummed his armrests apprehensively.

"Sequencing!" I hollered. "Going hypersonic!" The drives ramped into a high pitch as we watched the Moria Balá blow up…

…"HYPERSONIC ENABLED!" I flipped the toggles, reached down and jammed the trim levers forward, and the Zephyr left the chaos behind as she drove into the icy darkness. I adjusted our trajectory and sank into my seat as I put my headset back on and ran a systematic scan to check for damages.

I was thankful the Zephyr had redundant power source systems; with one of the main cryogen pipes that served the right hypersonic drive ruptured, I had to run a bypass to keep the drives operating. We were hit pretty bad, and I could only run them at three-quarter capacity or run the risk of squelching at full throttle.

I snickered as I shook my head and looked over at Scotty.

"Nikki, ya done good!" Scotty smiled as he exhaled loudly.

"We'll be at Ceres Vesta in about an hour."

"Then?"

"At the speed were going, we'll be minutes away from the Pipe."

"That was a hell of an experience."

"It was nothing compared to where we're heading." I nodded. "Scotty, why didn't you get in the pod and eject?"

"Not my style, Nikki. I couldn't leave someone like you behind to face those bandits alone."

"Thank you." I leaned over and kissed his cheek. "It's nice to know there's someone watching my back."

"You're welcome." Scotty blushed. "Don't get campy on me young lady. I don't want to get misty-eyed."

"You know, I've dealt with hijackers before but never face-to-face like that. I've always been able to outrun them."

"Nasty bunch, but I think it's safe to say we won't be seeing them again."

"We can always hope."

The Ceres Vesta asteroid belt was just ahead of us, and we could see thousands of rocks, chucks of ice, and wreckage from freighters floating by as we cut through the blue and yellow ion clouds that saturated the belt. Ceres Vesta's outer fringe was a graveyard for freighters and transports.

"Is that it?" Scott gawked. "Is that the pipe?"

"Not yet. Ceres Vesta is part of the Pipe's spin, the field is so dense that most flights avoid this sector because of the obvious threat of collusion with debris or a stone. The only ships that venture this close are usually salvage rats and platinum miners."

"If there are salvage and mining teams working this area, don't you think one of them would have discovered that pipe by now?"

"Yes, you would think so, but the pipe shows up on scanners as a magnetic anomaly--a huge one. I think the reason everyone avoids the inside region of Ceres Vesta is because the emissions are so strong that pilots think it will fry their instruments."

"Will it?"

"More than likely."

"Has it fried the Zephyrs in the past?"

"No."

"Why not?"

"I don't know. May be they're protected by the drive's fields."

"How close are we?"

"Take a look at the VDU and vector scanner." I pointed. "See that void the asteroid field is rotating around?"

"Yes."

"That's a ghost cavity. It's the center of the wormhole. We're fifteen minutes away from the Outer Horizon. In two minutes we'll be entering its jet at a seventy degree angle." I concentrated on dodging the husk of a large freighter that was adrift. "When we hit the barrier you're going to feel some turbulence when we merge into the stream. Don't panic, it's just tidal gravitational force. I'm going to throttle-up and we're going with the flow."

Scotty was silent again. He gazed at the passing ion clouds as we neared the Pipe's jet.

"I'm going to need you to stay calm, Scotty," I said reassuringly, "especially when we breach the Event Horizon and push into Singularity; you're going to feel a little strange on a physiological level, but don't freak out, okay?"

"What do you mean by "feel a little strange"?"

"I don't know how to explain it. It's just an eerie sensation, and your eyes may play tricks on you. It's not unpleasant, it's just different. Are you ready?"

"I can hardly wait."

"Don't be a wiseass. Brace yourself, we enter the jet in 4...3...2...1...and..."

The Zephyr reeled sideways and the cabin lights blinked as we were rocked in our seats. I pushed the levers on the center console slowly forward and ramped the drives up, they were almost at a hundred percent capacity, and I was comforted by their drone as the ship stabilized. I quietly stared out the canopy at the thin layers of ions in their shimmering blue dance against the darkness as we entered the Pipe's jet.

"Outer event in ten." I dimmed the overhead lights. "Romantic, eh?" I smiled.

"Who's being the wiseass now?"

"Clearly you can't be talking about me?" I said innocently.

"You've come a long way from that farm, Nikki. Can I ask you something?"

"As long as I don't have to answer it." I smirked.

"How did you get into this line of work?"

"There was a guy I used to date a couple of years ago. He was a weapons runner. His lifestyle fascinated me. He made a lot of money with every run, and his stories were exciting. He was exciting. The places he'd been, and the people he'd met. I wanted that life--that excitement. I wanted that edge."

"Are you still together?"

"He vanished over a year ago. No one knows what happened to him. Possible hijacking by pirates."

"Sorry Nikki."

"Don't worry about it. He knew the risks that came with the job."

"And still you do this?"

"It's all about the edge." I grinned. "Here we go..."

Date: 6-24-2408 / Time: 01300 hours / Velocity: 4.43HsD

...I reached down again and pulled the drive levers back to trim their thrust output. We were already accelerating at an alarming rate in the jet. A huge blackness defined itself ahead of us, its border was illuminated by thousands of points of light in a rapid orbit...

...the instrument panels began to flicker as alarms sounded off with a loud buzz. There seemed to be a hollow reverberation ringing throughout the bridge--a loud humming noise that consumed the senses...

Date: 6-24-2408 / Time: 01307 hours / Velocity: 5.8HsD

...the Zephyr had surpassed the maximum escape velocity she could do under her own power; we were now at the mercy of the Pipe. The ion clouds were gone, and we were engulfed in darkness and being pulled into the great void...

...the points of light outside began to merge as they passed by in streaks. Outer event had been penetrated, and we were still accelerating...

Date: 6-24-2408 / Time: 01309 hours / Velocity: 7.3HsD

...the gyroscope began to spin wildly as we breached the Inner Horizon. The scanners were glitching on and off, and there was an immense silence that pervaded the cockpit. The hum of the drives, the beeps and buzzes of audio alarms, and the dull drone of the O_2 generators--all sounds were pulled into total silence.

Read-outs on the VDU's were frozen, and all the loose gear in the overhead stowage racks drifted to the ceiling...my fedora floated off the console...

Date: 6-24-2408 / Time: 01309 hours / Velocity: 9.25HsD

...we punched through the photon sphere of the Event Horizon and the lighting in the bridge took on a surreal tint; a diffused glow that cast strange shadows on the walls, like the peculiar shadows that one only sees during an eclipse. Other worldly. Even the lights of the instrument panels glittered brighter than normal...

...I had the sensation of being stretched, and when I looked up at the cockpit canopy, I saw the back of my own head...

Date: 6-24-2408 / Time: 01309 hours / Velocity: unknown

...everything seemed distorted as we approached the center...Singularity. It was difficult for me to focus my eyes and I felt like I was suspended in time...the hallucination of being frozen against a wall of ice--cold and unattached to my body.

There was no gravitational force and yet everything felt like it was being pulled in the same direction...everything seemed warped...floating aimlessly through time. I turned and told Scotty we were almost there, but I couldn't hear my voice. The cabin and panel lights had blacked-out and we were in complete darkness.

The Pipe was quiet. Dead quiet.

Suddenly, everything snapped back on, the cabin lights illuminated the bridge, and everything that was floating dropped to the floor. There was a blinding flash of light, and I held up my hands to shield my eyes. A split second, and I was pushed into my seat hard.

The alarms blared as I grabbed the yoke, and the Zephyr rattled. I looked up just in time to see the Medusa system ahead. The gravity fields of the Pipe launched us through space like a marble fired from a slingshot, and within a matter of seconds we punched through Medusa's heliosphere.

I began a vector scan to confirm our trajectory to Nexus as I stabilized the Zephyr. To our right, we saw Jain 134; a huge blue-green planet with four moons. It was gorgeous and I could see the rays of Medusa's sun pierce its horizon as we passed.

"Scotty, are you okay?"

"I can't believe we're alive." Scotty gazed through the canopy and sank into his seat.

"Four minutes to Nexus. I hope Kurlie's people are paying attention."

"Just like that? We're actually in a different solar system now?"

"Yes, we're in Medusa, over three parsecs from home." I replied.

"How long would this flight have taken if we didn't go through that wormhole?"

"About ten weeks, give or take a few days, depending on our speed. A definite hypersleep voyage."

Scotty looked at his wristwatch. "Do you realize it's still the same time now that it was when we were on the other side of that thing?"

"So what's your point?"

"Just a thought, but did it ever occur to you that every time you went through the Pipe to shave weeks off your schedule that time froze for you?"

"Froze?"

"Yes, the ten weeks you just saved; I think you and I may not have aged, but everyone else did. Everyone we know is now ten weeks older."

"May be that's why things seemed a bit off with people whenever I got back from a run."

"It's a possibility."

"This conversation is making my head hurt, and your inner geek is showing. Are you always such a pain?"

We looked at each other and started laughing hard. We needed the levity badly. This was the only time I've had a passenger on a run, and I was glad I wasn't alone for the journey. Scotty had saved my life, and now he saved my sanity.

Nexus filled the canopy. It was a little larger than Earth but had two moons. I've always been struck by the view of planets from space; seeing the landmasses that made continents beneath the swirl of clouds within its atmosphere from afar was my favorite part of every flight.

I lit the thrusters and ramped down the drives. The sound of the rockets was always a welcome noise to me. I brought the Zephyr out of hypersonic flight as we eased into Nexus' exosphere where a blue halo surrounded the planet. We were traveling at Mach 6 and I held us in a high orbital pass over the hemisphere that was just receiving the first rays of morning light.

I retracted the hypersonic drive spawnsons and engaged the heat shields. "It's late afternoon in Fluture right now. We'll be dropping into atmosphere once I pick up the signal from Kurlie's clients. They'll give us the final coordinates for landing. Better put our flight helmets back on."

"Because of the nature of this flight, I'll assume we're not going to land at Fluture Stellar?"

"Probably not, but you never know with these people."

I checked the scanners when the VDU lit up and the image of an older man with dark hair and glasses appeared. He had a headset on with a small microphone, and his expression was solemn.

"Blue Zephyr, copy."

"Roger, Blue Zephyr copies." I responded dryly.

"I have you on panel. Confirm identification: "Swamp".

"Blue Zephyr confirms: "Fever".

"Welcome to Nexus, Ms. Wells. You should be receiving a beacon transmission in a moment. Set your final coordinates to that point. You are thirty-five hundred miles northwest of Fluture. Drop your speed to Mach 4 and maintain your altitude. Have you received the transmission?"

"Got it!" I smiled. "Transmission received and coordinates plotted." I disengaged the autopilot and slowly began to decelerate.

"Very good Zephyr. Maintain course until further instruction."

"10-4. Thank you, Fluture."

I exhaled and enjoyed the warmth of the sunlight. Within the hour, the Zephyr would be over the North Icarus continent and entering twilight as we neared the city.

"Are you going to have a place to stay when you get there?"

"Yes. Everything has been arranged for me. How about you?"

"I've got to tend to the damages to my ship. I'll figure it out from there, but I am planning on hitting the dance clubs." I glanced slyly at Scotty. "Think you'll have time to join me some time?"

"I'll be around." Scotty smiled as he turned his attention to his SCaT Pad.

The VDU chirped again, and our contact reappeared. "Blue Zephyr, copy."

"Blue Zephyr copies."

"Drop altitude to forty-five thousand feet and change heading to thirty-three minutes southwest."

The signal from the beacon grew stronger as we descended rapidly through the troposphere. It was a clear evening and there was a slight breeze coming from the east. I turned on the composite satellite image of the terrain below us as I made the changes to our flight path as instructed.

"Blue Zephyr, drop your altitude to fifteen thousand feet, bring your airspeed to subsonic, and hold your course."

"10-4 Fluture, fifteen thousand feet." The sky took on a gold and blue tint as the sun dipped below the horizon and gave the windswept clouds the violet color of evening. We were over a mountainous region, and we quietly looked at the shadows stretching over the landscape as Fluture city lights appeared in the distance.

"Zephyr, drop down to forty-three hundred feet and drop your speed to four hundred knots."

"Roger, forty-three hundred." I responded as I nosed the ship down.

Less than a minute later, the blue running lights of a runway appeared just outside city limits.

"Zephyr, you should have a visual on the landing strip from your position, please confirm."

"10-4, Fluture, I have a visual and have initiated final approach sequence." I glanced at Scotty and nodded.

"Adjust airspeed to three hundred knots."

"Welcome to Nexus." I smiled as I pushed forward on a lever to my left that lowered the landing gear. "Looks like we're setting down in a mining colony."

"How far are we from the city?"

"Not far, about sixteen kilometers."

"I'm going to have to make arrangements for transportation when we land."

"Fluture. That's a beautiful name for a city."

"It's Romanian." Scott smiled back. "The founder of the city, Dimitrie Lascăr, was from a European continent on Earth. Fluture means butterfly."

"The city's named Butterfly?"

"Yes. The area that Fluture was built on is actually the breeding grounds for a species of butterfly called the Blue Morphus Luna Didius. It's the largest butterfly known to man. Every five years, millions of Didius migrate here to mate. It's a spectacular event to witness."

"Why here?"

"It's the fauna. Their larva feed on a variety of plants that can only be found in several places on Nexus. The Didius that come here were born here. After their metamorphosis, they make a twenty-five hundred mile journey to a coastal region where they spend nine months. When they come back to Fluture, they mate, lay their eggs, then fly lack to the southern coast to die."

"How do you know all this?"

"I'm a genius." Scotty smirked. "This is the year for the Didius to return to Fluture. Maybe we'll get to see them."

"Blue Zephyr," our contact said briskly, "once you touch down, full reverse on your thrusters. The landing strip is only a mile and a half long."

"Shit!" I laughed and shook my head. "It's always something."

"Is this a problem?"

"We'll be okay…" I grinned, "…trust me."

"Good god."

We could see a huge mining site sprawled ahead as we made our approach. Wide dirt roads crisscrossed for miles in the darkening landscape that had been scarred by intense excavations. Heavy earth-moving equipment dotted the ground and the silhouettes of conveyor systems in steel trestles loomed in the darkness as we neared the landing strip.

There were hundreds of white, three story tilt-slab apartments, and dozens of glass office buildings that stretched for at least five miles on the western border of the mines. There was also what appeared to be a water treatment plant seated on the southern portion of the colony along with a series of process facility buildings, warehouses, and bulk chemical tanks.

I centered the Zephyr between the running lights of the strip and brought the nose up ten degrees. The thrusters droned heavily, and I extended the leading edges of the wings and rear stabilizers along with the air brakes to slow our descent as I lit up the high intensity beams under the fuselage and wings to illuminate the terrain in front of us.

We touched down with a slight bump as the main landing struts absorbed the force, and the nose wheel made contact with the steel tarmac. I reached down and pushed the trim levers forward steadily and began reverse thrust with the engines.

The Zephyr barreled past the small control tower of the landing strip, when I deployed a drag chute and put the thrusters in full reverse; the engines screamed and we were pushed forward against our seat harnesses as the ship vibrated hard and came to a slow taxi.

We came to a full stop at the edge of the airstrip where steel deflector barriers lined the perimeter. I could see the high grass in front of us being blown flat from our jets when I ramped them down to a five percent thrust and turned the Zephyr around a hundred and eighty degrees. A pilot truck pulled in front of us with its lights blinking and we were flanked on both sides by two black FAV's as we taxied forward.

The VDU blinked and our host appeared once again. "Bravo, Zephyr." The man smiled widely. "A well-executed landing on your part Ms. Wells. Please follow the truck to the designated hanger. Welcome to Cybelle."

Chapter 8

I shut the thrusters down when we reached the area by the control tower where a crawler latched on to us, and we were towed into a brightly lit hanger. I removed my helmet, set it on top of the instrument panel, and sighed with relief.

When we came to a full stop, I shut down all the systems and subsystems and depressurized the bridge and cargo bay. I stood up and put on my jacket and fedora and stretched my arms.

"What do you think, Scotty?"

Scott grabbed his gear and looked at me sternly as he put away his SCaT Pad. "Thanks for the ride Nikki," he smiled shyly as he shouldered his pack, "I'll see you back here in five days, okay?"

"Five days," I replied, "and don't be late." I opened the rear cargo doors and dropped the loading ramp.

When we stepped out of the Zephyr, we were met by the passengers of the FAV's. Rough looking bunch. One of them was clean-cut, bald, and well-dressed. He wore a dark suit and stood confidently among his cronies at the bottom of the ramp.

Scotty and I walked down the ramp and watched in silence as the suit lit a cigarette and inspected the Zephyr, he shook his head as he ran his hand over the tears and holes in the panels. "Jesus." He shot me a hard look. "You're the pilot?"

"Yes I am." I sighed as I gazed up at the thrashed vertical rudder.

"I see your ship has incurred some damage."

"We ran into some trouble on the way here. Pirates tried to hijack us, it's the reason we didn't get here sooner."

"What system did this happen in?" He frowned.

"Doesn't matter. We took care of them." I said coldly. "Can you recommend any aerospace mechanics?"

A moment later, two forklifts pulled up followed by a small crew of workers that gathered around us. They stood in a loose group and peered into the ship's hold.

The man in the suit clapped his hands and barked, "Okay boys, you know the drill. Let's get the merchandise off-loaded." He turned to one of the drivers, "Flynn, get the containers to the staging area and start an inventory. I'll contact Charon and let him know that they've arrived on time."

The driver nodded silently and looked at me. "Is the overhead crane in your ship operable?"

"Yes sir."

"May I?"

"Certainly. Careful with the handle for the trolley--it sticks sometimes."

"One moment please." The suit crushed his cigarette and pulled out his phone. "Mr. Charon, Jase. Yes sir, the product is here. It's being brought to the staging area as we speak. I'll call you back with a full inventory when Flynn's done. By the way, the pilot's ship took some damage from hijackers during the voyage. Yes sir, I'll let them know." Jase put his phone away. "When did you plan to depart?"

"Five days from now...the 29th."

"Your ship will be ready by then. Please make yourself available to answer any questions the mechanics and technicians may have concerning the Zephyr."

"I'm prepared to pay for the repairs."

"My employer will take care of the repairs for your ship."

The suit walked up to us and extended his hand. "I think a formal introduction is overdue. I'm Jase."

"Nikki Wells." I said with a nod as I shook his hand.

"Fenmore Scott." Scotty volunteered.

"We've made accommodations for both of you here at Cybelle. I think you'll find your apartments quite agreeable and your stay pleasant."

"That's very generous of you, Mr. Jase," Scotty said, "but I've already made provisions in Fluture."

"As you wish." Jase bowed. "I'll arrange for your transportation to the city. "I have to admit, Ms. Wells," Jase smiled, "I was skeptical about your ability to hit the schedule when I was told you left Earth six days ago."

"It's been a hell of a journey."

"Looks like it. Let's get you settled in."

Scotty and I exchanged SP numbers as I threw my gear in one of the FAV's.

A black Avarno SS-2 sedan pulled up to us and the driver got out and handed Scotty the keys.

"Nice ride, Scotty."

"You'll be okay Nikki?"

"Yeah, I can handle things on my end." I glanced at the FAV driver that was waiting for me. "What about you?"

Scott smiled wordlessly as he put his bags in the passenger seat of the car, slid into the driver's side, and fired up the vehicle. He nodded at me then drove into the night.

Charon moved through the crowded floor of the casino accompanied by two bodyguards. He enjoyed mingling with the clientele and checking in with the dealers on busy nights like this, it gave him a chance to press the flesh and see everything in action. This was his business now, and he liked to be as hands-on as possible.

It's been three hours since he talked to Jase and he wondered what the status was with his purchase. He spent a lot of money on this product and he was concerned about Montrell's ability to deliver. If he got burned on this deal, he would see to it that Montrell suffered.

He sighed with relief when his phone rang, and saw that it was Jase. "It's about time. What's going on Jase?" Charon said impatiently.

"Sorry for the delay, Mr. Charon, we had to make sure everything was copasetic, so we counted and weighed everything twice."

"And?"

"All three thousand gallons of isomerized Beta-ephedrine are accounted for, they came in five-gallon containers beneath the cosmetics. Sorben tested random samples of the product and it's a hundred percent pure."

"Excellent, get the Beta-ephedrine palletized and to the lab as soon as possible. Looks like Montrell came through and is a man of his word."

"What do you want to do with the ship's crew? Shall we go ahead with the repairs?"

He was feeling unusually generous in light of the good news. "Nothing. They're Montrell's employees. They'll be useful to us again for the next delivery. Do whatever it takes to get their ship space worthy."

"What about the cosmetics?"

"Get them distributed to the call-out sites for the girls."

"Yes sir."

Charon hung up and smiled. Three thousand gallons. His production rate was going to escalate twenty-fold over the next few months, and his drug ring profit would grow exponentially once this new batch of Crunch hits the streets and mining colonies.

He walked up to a young woman wearing a silver gown with a plunging neckline. A choker made of blue Serenian pearls accented the curve of her neck and gave her an air of nobility. She was about eighteen years old and stood at a Black Jack table with a well-dressed man that was at least twice her age.

She was just fourteen years old when Charon found her. A runaway from Southern Icarus wandering the streets of Fluture; lost, confused, and desperate, she stood outside his casino spanging the customers when he saw her and took her under his protection from the nickel and dime urchins.

She was a petite 5'-4", with long brown hair and a dark complexion that brought out the color of her light blue eyes. Exotic. Her birth name was irrelevant now, to Charon and his clients, she was known only as Summer, and her time was worth a fortune.

"I want you at my table." Charon whispered in her ear as he put his hand on her shoulder.

"Now?" Summer asked demurely.

"Be ready in thirty minutes."

"Yes Mr. Charon." Summer smiled as she dismissed herself and headed up to her room.

Charon's bodyguards watched her disappear into the crowd then looked at each other deviously.

Summer was well cared for and her apartment was luxurious. She bought everything with her own money, and it was her sanctuary from her job--it was the one place they couldn't touch her, the only place she knew as home.

Her only wish was that one day she could leave this place and go far away from Fluture. Far away enough to forget this life and find herself peace and happiness. She could barely remember her old life before Charon; all there was were broken memories of an abusive step-father that used to beat her mother.

She remembered the blood-stained aprons and the blackened eyes on her mother when she got home from school...the falling down the stairs excuse was never a convincing story. Especially when *he* would be passed-out on the living room couch from another alcohol-induced coma.

She hated him for what he did, and she often tried to persuade her mom to leave before she ended up dead.

But it was her that ran, under the cover of night, she packed a small bag, stole the cash out of his billfold, and hitched out of the house without looking back. She would never look back.

She turned heads as she glided through the hotel lobby and stepped into the glass elevator that would take her to the fourteenth floor apartment. Summer turned around and clutched her small purse as she watched the glimmering city lights below as the elevator rose.

She surveyed her studio as she walked in and turn on some music. Summer sat in front of her vanity and reapplied her lipstick as she checked her hair and eye shadow. She sat quietly and opened a drawer where she pulled out a small mirror and razorblade and set them on the counter.

She reached into her purse, took out a small glass vile, and emptied some of its contents on the mirror where she started chopping-up the white powder with the razor. It was a regrettable ritual. Summer pushed the Crunch into a line, took a short glass tube, leaned down, and inhaled it quickly. When she looked at her reflection again, she was crying.

"**J**esus Christ this bird's been through some shit!" The mechanic cussed as a half-chewed cigar dangled from his lips. He rubbed the back of his head as he looked over the fuselage of the Zephyr. "Look at the farking hole in this panel!" He pointed. "What the hell did that?"

"Nevermind what did that, can you fix this within four days or not? I'm looking to head back to Earth by then."

"Yeah, yeah, it's doable, girlie." The mechanic exhaled. "I'm going to have to purge the cryogen system in order to cut out and replace the punctured section of that twenty inch main."

"But it's got a bypass."

"Oh yeah. I can see it now," he gestured as he pulled the stogie out of his mouth, "I strike an arc, it ignites residual cryogen gas, and blows my ass up to the back of my neck."

"But you've got hair on the back of your neck."

"Then I guess I'm gonna have a hairy ass after the explosion."

I looked away trying not to laugh. "What do you think?"

"Don't worry young lady, the guys and I will have your ship tooled and fueled in three days."

"Hey, where can a girl go to have some fun around here?"

"You plan on going to the city?"

"Absolutely."

"Ya got a way to get there?"

"Not at the moment."

He squinted at me and shook his head. "Space jockey." He smirked. "Follow me." He led me down a corridor to another part of the hanger. "What's your name anyway, girlie?"

"Nikki."

"Pleased to meet'cha. I'm Doolie. I'm the master mechanic in this facility. The boss said to take care of you, so here we are." He turned on the bay lights in a workshop and there were six cars parked tightly in a garage. "Take your pick. They're all loaners reserved for special guests."

"How about that one?" I pointed at a black racing bike sitting in the corner.

"That's a Neko A3 Cyclone."

"Yeah, it sure is." I smiled. "Otherwise known as The Cat."

Doolie rolled his eyes as he pulled the keys off a pegboard mounted on the wall and tossed them to me. "Space jockey." He grinned. "Have fun in Fluture."

"Meow!" I winked as I slipped on the helmet.

Chapter 9

Fluture was truly the city of lights on Nexus; beautiful, overpowering, and restless, I could almost feel the pulse of the city as I watched the sidewalks swarming with people prowling through the lights in the nightly hunt for the next thrill in their lives in the concrete jungle.

The boulevard was lined with clubs, casinos, and luxury highrises that towered over the mass of activity. Brightly decorated banners with tiny blue and white lights were strung overhead and declared this year as "The Year of the Butterfly". Scotty was right, the migration of the Didius was an event not to be missed in Fluture.

The neon lights of the main drag flashed in a kaleidoscope of brilliant colors as I cruised along with stretch-limousines, taxi cabs, and flashy status symbols of the ultra-rich. This was the city where fortunes were made and lost in seconds, and lives hinged on fate and luck.

The casino I was looking for was just up ahead--The Orchid was the largest and most lavish structure there; it was the diamond of Fluture nightlife. There were huge fountains with waterfalls in the center of the porte cochère where guests pulled up and were greeted by smartly dressed valets constantly hustling to park their cars or open the doors of the limos to usher in the highrollers and celebrities.

This was the place where the rich and famous came to be seen, adored, and envied. The Orchid was where money worshipped the face of youth with extravagance and excess.

I pulled in on the Cyclone and idled in front of the main entrance when a valet in a red jacket jogged up to me. "Excuse me sir, you'll have to park over there." He pointed to a gated area where about forty motorcycles were grouped for the evening. "I can take your personal items and helmet after you find a spot." He smiled warmly.

I nodded silently at the valet and gunned the Cat to the designated space and shut it off. I opened the small storage compartment behind the seat and grabbed my silver clutch bag and headed toward the lobby.

My bomber jacket was zipped up, and I was wearing the HUD helmet with a reflective face shield that came with the Cyclone along with black leather pants, gloves, and cowboy boots.

I walked up to the podium to the left of the grand entryway where the valets gathered and tracked guest keys and personal belongings. The one that greeted me smiled as he approached. I removed the helmet and shook my hair loose so that it fell to my shoulders. He looked at me with surprised embarrassment when he realized I was female.

"Gosh, I'm so sorry I called you sir!" He blushed.

"No worries." I handed him my helmet and gloves. "Do you mind?" I asked as I reached over and positioned his arms higher so that I could see my reflection on the helmet visor. I opened my clutch, pulled out my lipstick, and leaned forward to reapply it. When I finished, I put it back and patted the valet on his blushing cheek. "I'll be back in a few hours," I smiled, "take good care of my stuff, okay?"

"Yes ma'am!" He bowed.

A red carpet led through the entrance to the lobby, and once inside, I was awed by three crystal chandeliers that spiraled from the cathedral ceilings and centered over a huge, blue orchid that was designed into the white terrazzo floor. The orchid itself was a marvel to look at; it was at least thirty feet in diameter, and the petals and sepals were composed of five different shades of blue. It was a breathtaking centerpiece.

The blue and white marble walls were complimented by thousands of silver and white butterfly ornaments that cascaded from the ceiling between the split staircases that curved up to the mezzanine.

Flower arrangements made of the different species of orchids that grew in Fluture were everywhere, and visitors and guests milled around and mingled as servers circulated with bottles of campaign and silver platters of carefully arranged hors d'oeuvres. This place was gorgeous and aimed to overindulge Fluture's power players with its luxurious atmosphere.

I wove casually through the groups of people until I spotted a crowd gathered at the main entrance of a nite club called the Electric Gypsy. There were a couple of huge doormen in black suits that stood in front pointing at certain patrons and waved them in past the velvet ropes when I edged forward to take a closer look.

"You, you, and you, may come in." One of them bellowed as he unhitched a chain that symbolically divided people by their appearance.

"Aw come on!" A man in his early thirties whined. "What's it going to take to gain admission? Is it money you want? Credits?"

A bouncer glared at him. "It's not about money, it's about the energy. Only people with the groove get in."

"What the hell are you talking about?" The man demanded in an incensed tone.

"Those who know don't tell, those who tell don't know. If you have to ask, then you don't need to know." The bouncer stepped forward and pushed him back into the crowd. "You and you," he gestured at two girls standing in front of me, "may enter."

They looked at each other and squealed in delight as they clapped their hands and went down the stairs that led to the underground club.

The bouncer looked at me and a blonde girl wearing a short white cocktail dress standing to my right, "You and you," he pointed, "may enter." He said gruffly as he unhitched the chain and ushered us toward the brightly lit stairwell where another man stood at the bottom in front of a second entrance.

I could hear the beat of techno-trance pounding through the heavy doors and the cheering of hundreds of voices.

"Welcome to the Electric Gypsy." The doorman nodded as he let us into a vast, darkened ballroom. The party was packed and in full swing. The center of the room had an elevated circular platform that was twenty feet in diameter, where the DJ and technicians controlled everything that created the hypnotic atmosphere of flashing lights and lasers.

I started moving my shoulders instinctively to the seductive beat of the bass drum and synthesizers as I melted into the mob. I was automatically drawn to the platform, and people rubbed against me as I danced through the bodies moving rhythmically with the beat.

The DJ wore a red and white striped stovepipe hat and a head-mic, and he moved over a large console flipping switches to create electronic sounds that kept the music going. His face and body were chalk-white, and red theatrical make-up was applied in a wild design on his face that accented his mouth and eyes and made him look like an evil clown.

His falsetto voice reverberated with the synthesizers and bass beat as he sang the club's theme song:

Ten thousand light years
I've roamed the skies
I've touched the rainbow
and it feels like ice
I move so fast,
never touch the ground
I live my life at the speed of sound...

...the crowd danced wildly to the anthem and pumped their fists in the air as they sang along at the top of their lungs...

Techno-Gypsy, Electric Gypsy
The night is young,
Gypsy, Oh Electric Gypsy
All night long

...the laser lights pulsed red and blue rays from the platform as the silhouettes of clubbers waved glow sticks, squirted water bottles, and jumped up and down in unison...screaming...

I won't come down
so don't make me try
My sonic dream
is never gonna die
I'll take my chances
on chrome and steel
Live fast die young is how I feel...

Techno-Gypsy, Electric Gypsy
The night is young,
Gypsy, Oh, Electric Gypsy
All night long

The DJ came down from the platform and started dancing with a group of girls. He was wearing tight red vinyl pants and undulated with the music as the girls ran their hands over his pale shirtless body.

The girl I came in with shrieked, "OH HERRON, YOU'RE GOD! I LOVE YOU!" And the DJ spun several times and floated to where we were dancing.

"Trance is energy, baby." He purred. "Are you here with anyone?"

She shook her head and beamed.

"Perfect!" He smiled widely. "Give yourself to me tonight."

He took her hand and led her to the platform. The group of girls he danced with clawed at him for attention, but a couple of bouncers stepped in and yanked them away. The DJ had made his choice and brought the girl to the stage and started manipulating the console again as she stood star-struck and watched her idol in fascination.

Even through the chaos of strobe lights, and the echo of electronic voices inducing the frenzy of sweat and hypnotic lust, I saw the DJ hand the girl a small vile and encourage her to inhale its contents while she danced seductively to the music. Crunch dust.

The ceiling burst with blinding white light and flickered back to darkness as the techno-trance engulfed the crowd and electrified the air. Someone handed me a bottle of water and motioned for me to drink it. I handed it back and moved through the mass of howling people indulging themselves in the scene as a giant blue butterfly appeared and floated gracefully over the horde of clubbers.

I made my way to the side of the dance floor and looked for an empty seat at the tables that were set up for spectators on a raised floor. I moved through the mingling people watching the bash when I spotted a small, empty table by the handrail that bordered the floor perimeter. I sat down and exhaled and watched the butterfly glide over the party.

"It's a great scene isn't it?" A man with long dark hair wearing a vest and dark glasses sat down and edged up next to me.

"Yes it is."

"I'm Roscoe Brown, the ladies call me RB." He said smoothly as he dropped his voice an octave.

I recognized the approach. "I'm not really looking for any company, handsome." I said politely.

"Hey, you need to get hooked up? I can get you anything. You need some crunch? Psycho-dots? How about some Afterburner?"

"No thanks, I'm not into getting chemically motivated to do something stupid." I frowned as I turned my attention back to the dance floor.

"How about me then?" He grinned.

"Huh?"

"Want to session?" He stood up and rubbed the bulge in his crotch. "I can promise you a night you'll never forget."

I rolled my eyes in disgust. "I've seen bigger balls on a kitten. Do yourself a favor and give those steamed clams the night off, handsome."

"You keep calling me handsome, so there's obviously something about me you like."

"I call you handsome because you're going home alone tonight and going to be using your hand-some."

Roscoe laughed and put his hand on my lap as he sat back down. "I bet you like it rough, am I right?" He squeezed my thigh and ran it a little higher. "I bet you can get real nasty with the right man." He winked.

I laughed along with him as I reached down, grabbed his hand, and set it flat on the table. "Oh Roscoe," I smiled as I reached over and removed his sunglasses and put them on, "you definitely have a way about you, and you're right, I can get *real* nasty."

He smiled confidently and tilted his head sideways and eyed my breasts.

"I tell you what," I said with a softer voice as I lightly stroked the wrist of his hand on the table, "I'm going to get you something to drink..." I leaned in and slipped my other hand into his vest without him noticing and removed the stiletto he had stashed in the right pocket.

"...while you sit here and try to figure out..." I held the knife up in front of his face, flicked the switch that snapped the blade out, and watched his eyes widened as I drove it hard through the top of his hand and pegged it to the table, "...how this evening could have turned out better for you."

"SON-OF-A-BITCH! GET THIS OFF OF ME!" He screamed as he stared in shock at his impaled hand.

"Don't go anywhere, I'll be right back." I got up and went to the bar.

Summer sat in a corner booth and watched Roscoe whimpering as the girl with the leather jacket stood up and calmly walked away. A crowd was gathering around him as he cringed and yelled for help.

She got up to see what the commotion was all about; when she got to Roscoe's table, she saw a growing pool of blood and a stiletto knife jammed through the top of his hand.

"Don't just stand there you idiots, get some help!" Roscoe screamed. "Summer! You little whore! Get me some help, damn it!" He demanded as he looked helplessly at his injury and pounded his fist on the tabletop in agony.

Summer had a hard time concealing her smile. "Having a bad night, Roscoe?" She reached down and wiggled the handle of the knife.

"YAAAAH! DON'T TOUCH IT! DON'T TOUCH IT!" He cried hysterically.

"Excuse me. Pardon me. I'm sorry, I just need to get through for a second." Nikki nudged her way politely through the crowd standing around Roscoe's table. She had a pitcher of beer.

"Hi honey, I brought you something to drink." Nikki poured the beer on Roscoe's head, set the pitcher next to his bleeding hand, then punched him in the face with a straight left jab that knocked him out cold. His body slumped forward and his face hit the table hard. The crowd gasped and parted as Nikki turned around and walked to the restroom wearing Roscoe's sunglasses.

Summer watched her walk away coolly and admired her confidence. She looked at the mess that was Roscoe and decided to follow her. When she got to the ladies room, she saw Nikki washing blood off her hands in the clam-shaped sink.

Summer smiled coyly and nodded as they made eye contact, and took the spot next to Nikki and pretended to fix her hair. It took a few seconds to work up the courage to say something, and she tried not to be distracted by the bloody water spinning down the drain as she watched Nikki scrub her hands clean.

She side-eyed Nikki in the mirror. "That guy you hammered back there...do you know who he is?"

"He said his name was Roscoe." Nikki shrugged as she reached for a towel.

"Roscoe Brown is one of the biggest drug dealers in south Fluture." Summer said dryly. "A real balloon knot that walks around here like the world owes him a living."

"He struck me as a pathetic turd-slurper."

"He is."

The girls burst out laughing as they looked at their reflections in the mirror. Summer put her hand over her mouth and blushed as she shook her head.

"I've never heard that one before."

"Yeah, well, I have my moments."

"I'm Summer." She held out her hand and smiled.

"Nikki." She shook Summer's hand. "Is the Gypsy open every night?"

"It closes for three days every month for maintenance. Are you new to Fluture?"

"Just passing through." Nikki looked at Summer. "Lovely dress."

"Thank you. Where are you from?"

"Earth."

"I've heard of your planet, you're a long way from home."

"I sure am. I'm here on business. Now I'm here to take in the nightlife. Are you from Nexus?"

"Yes, I'm originally from Southern Icarus, but I live here in Fluture."

"You're a long way from home too. So what do you do?"

"I work here at the casino. How about you?"

"I'm a pilot."

"Really? You must see a lot of places. What company do you work for?"

"I'm on commission. I own my ship."

"Wow Nikki, if you don't mind my saying so, you are by far the most interesting girl I've ever met. You sound like you have an exciting life, and what you did to Roscoe out there was epic."

"Like I said, I have my moments." Nikki grinned.

"Do you want to hang out? May be get something to eat?"

"Sounds good. I'm famished." Nikki threw Roscoe's glasses in the trash bin as they stepped back out to the party.

They were met by two hulking men in black uniforms-- members of The Orchid's security team. Roscoe stood between them cradling his wrapped up hand. "That's her!" He scowled as he pointed at Nikki.

The security guards looked at each other, then at Nikki, "Young lady," one of them said calmly, "this man claims you assaulted him with a knife. Do you know him?"

"I beg your pardon?" Nikki feigned a look of confusion. "I've never seen this gentleman before. What happened?" She asked innocently.

"She's lying!" Roscoe barked. "You little bi..."

"She's with me." Summer intervened as she looked the security man square in the eyes. "She's an old friend of mine."

"She's lying too!" Roscoe spit venomously. His shirt was soaked with blood and his right eye was black.

The security guards glared at Roscoe then looked at Summer. "Mr. Charon's been wondering where you've been."

"I'm sorry, I lost track of time when I ran into Nikki. We haven't seen each other in years." Summer said apologetically as she hooked her left arm around Nikki's right. "Can you tell Charon I'll be up in a few minutes?"

"You've got ten minutes." The man said firmly. "Then you get your ass up there to join Charon for dinner. Don't make me come looking for you."

"Hey wait a minute," Roscoe contested, "what about her?" He pointed at Nikki.

"Nikki's been hanging with me all night," Summer piped as she looked at the security guards, "I have no idea what Roscoe's babbling about. He's probably drunk and hitting the crunch again. Look at him, he even spilled his drink all over himself."

The security guard slapped Roscoe on the side of the head. "Shut up, yhamo," the guard grunted in disgust, "I catch you in here with a knife again, I'm going to stick it up your ass. You hear me?" The guards turned and half dragged Roscoe away. "Now go put on your big boy pants and go upstairs and have a med-tech look at your hand."

Summer looked at Nikki. "I'm sorry, I have to go."

"Thanks for the cover story, Summer."

"May be I'll see you around."

Nikki watched Summer disappear into the crowd. She couldn't help but feel that the girl did her a big favor by standing up for her in front of the guards.

She sensed a certain sadness in Summer's eyes. Even though the girl was wearing a gown that probably cost thousands of dollars, there was an air of desperation about her. Especially when the guard told her she was late for some sort of dinner date.

It was getting late and Nikki decided to get back to Cybelle and get some rest. She had taken in enough action for the night and didn't want to push her luck.

As she made her way through the mob and passed by the platform, she saw the DJ still spinning his magic and strutting around, but the girl she had come in with was gone.

The next morning, Scott took a taxi to the business district of downtown Fluture from his hotel and left the SS-2 in the parking garage where the valet put it the night before. He got out and walked three blocks where he hailed another cab that took him to a mall. Scott walked around and settled into a crowded café where he ordered lunch and waited as he read his SCaT Pad.

Ten minutes later, a man in a tan jacket sat at the table next to him and ordered a cup of coffee. They never made eye contact or acknowledged each other's existence. The man read his newspaper as he casually sipped his beverage and regarded bypassers. When he was done, he folded his paper, stood up, and dropped it on Scott's table as he walked away without looking back.

Scott unfolded the paper to a set of car keys. There was also a hastily written address and a license plate number for a blue sedan. He got up, paid for his meal, and headed for the parking lot.

It took him a few minutes to find the car, but once he did, he was pleased by the banality of the vehicle. It was the type of car that had no character and anyone seen driving it would never raise suspicion. He got in and drove south for a half hour until he arrived to an industrial area on the edge of Fluture.

Scott made a right onto a desolate main street that ran between a series of buildings. He slowed down and leaned forward, hunting for the address as the afternoon shadows stretched across the potholed street and loose papers caught in a breeze blew across with wafts of dust.

The area was packed with abandoned warehouses and factories. Some of the street numbers were clearly visible on the structures, but most of the buildings weren't marked. Scott turned on his GPS and punched in the address as he cruised down the road. He spotted the building at the same time the GPS located it on a satellite map and started blinking. The structure was a dingy warehouse with broken windows, and the exterior walls were covered with graffiti.

Scott saw three cars parked in the alley next to it. He pulled in behind them, got out slowly, and walked to the front of the building. A door opened and two men stepped outside of the structure and looked at him suspiciously.

One had a thick mustache and wore a black tank top and jeans. His arms were sleeved with tattoos that ran up to his neck, and judging from the designs, he got them in prison. The other was heavyset and wore a gray jogging suit. He was adorned with thick gold chain necklaces and an obnoxious wrist watch that must have weighed two pounds.

"There something we can help you with, yhamo?" The one with a mustache asked with a low, threatening tone.

"Perhaps. I'm here to see Lazarus."

"Wass your name, yhamo?"

"Scott."

The two men looked at each other and nodded. The heavy one went inside the building while the other stood outside with Scott and glared at him.

A few seconds later, the heavy one poked his head out of the door and waved him in. The building was empty and cavernous. It was dim, dusty, and the lights glowed dully overhead as Scott followed the heavyset man inside while the tattooed one walked next to him.

There was a long table set up against the east wall with two black cases and a duffle bag on top. Scott noticed there were two other men holding automatic weapons standing at the end of a dark hallway watching him as he crossed the floor.

"Wait here." The heavy one ordered as he held up his hand. The one with the mustache stood next to him with his arms crossed.

A voice came out of the darkness. "So you're him. The one they call Scott."

Scott stood silently as he looked in the direction of the two armed men where the voice came from. A man wearing a dark gray suit stepped forward, walked over to the long table, and stood in the shadows.

"Come closer." He said calmly. "I think you'll find everything to your satisfaction."

"I trust that my employers have compensated you financially?" Scott asked as he approached the table.

"They have. Procurement of these items was difficult."

"Lazarus?"

"I am." The man leaned forward and stepped out of the gloom. His face was covered with scars and pitted heavily. His nose was also missing.

"Go ahead. Take a look." He pointed at the items on the table.

Scott opened the longer flat case and surveyed nine parts of various shapes and sizes that were held tightly in place by foam cushioning. He ran his fingertips lightly over the pieces that were matted in flat black, and could tell that they were products of precision tooling and engineering.

"May I?" Scott placed his hand on one of the components and pulled it out of the case.

"Try not to soil yourself." Lazarus chuckled.

It took less than a minute. Scott quickly picked the parts out one at a time and expertly began assembly as the others looked on. He snapped, tightened, and twisted the components and marveled at their fit as they began to take on the shape of a weapon. The others watched quietly as he scrutinized the last piece and slapped it into the receiver.

Scott grinned as he examined the fully assembled Trinity M341 SWS Rifle with flash and sound suppressor; the rifle's overall length was only thirty-two inches. Thirty-two inches of high-powered velocity capable of delivering death with surgical precision. He snapped the bolt back to check the action, then peered down the scope that had an anti-glare, infrared lens. The barrel was fourteen inches long with a vented heat shield. He held the weapon up and checked it's weight and balance. This thing was a demon. "I am become death." Scott thought to himself.

"You have six rounds." Lazarus said coldly. "Two armor-piercing hollow points, and four explosive--as you requested. I also got you the Kirsten Automatic Pistol with four-thirty round clips, and four Pyrogen fragmentation grenades." Lazarus slid the smaller case to Scott.

Scott disassembled the rifle and carefully put the parts back into the case. He reached for the Kirsten Auto and flicked the selector switch as he wrapped his fingers around the grip and pulled back the magazine catch spring and let it slap back into position.

"And last, but not least," Lazarus picked up a small duffle bag and set it in front of Scott. "there's six ounces of Black Swan with a transmitter and three detonation receiver rings wrapped in the ghillie suit along with the frags, a range finder, and an area map of Sertina's Pass."

Scott set the Kirsten Auto on the table, unzipped the bag, and unrolled the ghillie suit to inspect the items. "Excellent." He said dryly as he set the Kirsten and spare clips next to the range finder and detonation rings, rolled everything back up, and stuffed them back into the duffle. "Thank you, Lazarus. You are a great asset to this process."

"So, you never saw me, you don't know my name, and this meeting and conversation never took place. Understood?"

"Goes without saying."

Lazarus turned to his men. "Let's go." They surrounded him as they filed through the corridor. Lazarus paused, turned around, and looked at Scott. "Whatever it is you're here to do," Lazarus said grimly as one of his bodyguards stood next to him and stared coldly at Scott, "I have a feeling I'll be seeing it in the headlines."

Scott nodded stoically at him and they disappeared into the darkness. He watched them get into their cars and drive down the street where they took a left and vanished from sight. He sighed as he grabbed the case and shouldered the duffle bag; he had a few more things to do in the city, then had to go back to Cybelle to tie up a couple of loose ends.

I adjusted my fedora as I walked around the Zephyr and assessed the overall damage to my ship. Doolie had already set up a work station and the larger RAM panels that sustained the most damage had been stripped off and stacked neatly on a forklift.

There was a six-man crew of mechanics and technicians working on different parts of the ship; one of them was on a lift clamping off the control surface on the vertical rudder that was torn to shreds, and the others were either working on damaged wiring or replacing minor components on the Zephyr.

A couple of welding drones were in the process of reworking the omni-strut panel mounts that got torqued from the attack, and Doolie was doing the final testing and inspections on the quality of the work.

"Well good morning Nikki." Doolie removed his face shield and ducked under one of the ventral fins.

"I can't believe how fast you guys move on getting things done."

"We started last night after you left for the city."

"You mean you haven't slept yet?"

"Nope, we have direct orders from the man himself to do whatever it takes to get your ship repaired."

"Do you have all the parts you need to make the Zephyr space worthy?"

"I believe so. We still have to replace some sensors before putting on the new panels, but I'm happy with what we've accomplished so far. Some of the fiber optics got cooked, but it's no big deal, the techs are re-pulling them."

"Thanks Doolie, I appreciate how hard you and your crew have been working."

"No problem. It's what we do. I took a look at the major systems and avionic controls and everything checks out. That rudder is beat to shit though."

"It sure is." I stepped back to let one of the drones roll by.

"The subsystems in this baby are in excellent shape. I see you've got a lot of aftermarket parts and systems in your ship."

"I've had quite a bit of work done, and I did a lot of the system bashing myself."

"Nice." Doolie nodded admiringly. "I don't see magnetic hyper-drive cores very often, yet alone get the chance to work on them, so this is a nice break in routine."

"Is this going to cause problems?"

"Nothing we can't handle. We'll even replace the ceramic detonation ring on the docking collar." Doolie cleared his throat. "If you don't mind me asking, what happened?"

"Pirates tried to hijack us just outside of Tal-Seti. It got nasty and we got into it pretty bad with them."

"They still out there?"

"No, we managed to take care of them."

Doolie rubbed his chin and squinted. "You know, Jase has been down here three times to see how the repairs are going. He's rarely at port for anything, but he wants your vessel operational as soon as possible."

"Can't wait to get rid of me already?"

"No, nothing like that young lady. I'm assuming he and Mr. Charon are pleased with the quality of the merchandise and your ability to make the schedule. From the way Jase talks, looks like I'll be seeing more of you around here."

"What do you mean?"

"I think after two or three more runs Mr. Charon may bring you in full time."

"Full time? Oh no, no, no!" I shook my head. "There's got to be some sort of miscommunication between your boss and mine, this was a one-time deal."

Doolie chuckled. "Nikki, you stand to make a lot of money bringing in more Beta-ephedrine."

I tried not to act surprised by what Doolie just said, so just I stood there quietly and listened.

"That batch you delivered was serious Grade-5 Beta-E." Doolie whistled. "One hundred percent pure. The guys at the lab are still talking about it."

"They are, huh?"

I wondered what this beta stuff was used for. My mind drifted...damn it, Kurlie lied to me. I told him no drugs! I didn't want to ask Doolie what this stuff was since he assumed I knew what he was talking about.

"Absolutely. Jase was thinking about bringing you in every three to four months depending on the demand, so it looks like we'll be servicing your ship every time you make a drop."

"I wasn't planning on making any more trips to Nexus after this one, Doolie."

"That's between you and the man."

"Is there a way you can arrange for me to talk to this Charon?"

"That's above my pay grade. You'll have to take that up with Jase. Hey, if it makes you feel any better, you can use the Cyclone every time you come to Nexus."

"I'm going to have to think about this." I muttered.

"You wanna take a look around?"

"Am I allowed to?"

"I don't see why not. You're the one risking your ass getting it here. Let me give you a quick tour of the joint."

"Sure why not?" I thought this might be a good opportunity to gain some insight on what Doolie was talking about.

Cybelle was a huge mining colony but apparently it was used as a front for purposes other than mining. We hopped into an FAV and went to the warehouse that the cargo was brought to. The containers were empty now, and the cosmetics were still being palletized, but the beta-ephedrine was gone.

Whatever I brought to Nexus seemed to be a big deal and was part of a larger process. That would explain why everyone moved so fast when it came to the offloading, inventory, and distribution of the payload.

I'm going to have a sit down with Kurlie when I get back home and find out what he got me into. I was under the impression that he made some promises to people here that involved me, and my plans on throwing in the towel were about to be altered.

"So where did the Beta-E go?" I asked.

"The labs on the west side of the facility. I'm afraid I can't take you there."

It was about noon when we got back to the hanger where the Zephyr was moored. To my surprise, Scotty had shown up and was looking around and watching the mechanics at work.

"Scotty!" I beamed as I hugged him.

"Hi Nikki." Scott smiled. "How's everything going here? Is everything all right? Are we still on schedule?"

"Yes." I said as I gestured at the Zephyr. "This is Doolie," I said formally, "he's the lead mechanic repairing my ship and the manager of this facility. Doolie, this is Scotty, my copilot."

"Nice to meet 'cha Scotty." Doolie shook Scott's hand. "Well, if you two will excuse me, I have to get back to work."

"Thanks for the tour, Doolie."

"My pleasure, Nikki."

"Scotty, what brings you back here?"

"I need a favor from you."

"Sure, what's up?"

"I've got some personal things I'd like you to hang on to until we meet up again." Scotty reached into his backpack and handed me his SCaT Pad and a small key. "I don't want to lose them in the city."

"Okay. Do you have time for lunch?"

"There somewhere around here to eat?"

"There's a restaurant at the complex I'm staying at. Can you give me a lift?"

"The car's parked just outside."

As we walked out of the facility, I couldn't shake the feeling of being watched as we approached the SS-2.

"What's on your mind, Nikki?"

"We need to talk."

"This sounds serious."

"It is. I just found out about something that I don't like."

"If that's the case, don't talk about it in the car. Wait until we get to the restaurant."

"You think the Avarno's bugged?"

"I didn't say that."

"But you suspect something."

"I suspect everything. There's no honor among people in this business. We'll talk about it over a decent meal."

We were seated in a corner booth by the hostess, and the moment she left, Scotty moved us to a table outside on the covered patio.

Scotty looked around and leaned back in his chair. "This is much better." He sighed as he looked at the sky and grinned. "So what's going on? How was your first night, did you get some rest or go to Fluture?"

"I went to the city. I was out pretty late last night. I see what you mean about these thirty-six hour days." I browsed through a menu for an entrée.

"Did you find a decent dance club?"

The waiter came and took our orders. "I went to a club at The Orchid."

"The Orchid is the swankiest casino in the city. I'm staying at the La Rouge Hotel there."

"Scotty, how well do you know Kurlie? I know I'm not supposed to ask, but I really need to know; do you work for him?"

"No, I don't work for Montrell any more than you do, he's just an acquaintance. Why?"

"Have you ever heard of Beta-ephedrine?"

"Yes I have, what about it?"

"Kurlie told me I was just delivering some high-dollar cosmetics and other luxury commodities. I should have known better than to believe him. Apparently there was a large amount of beta-ephedrine hidden in the cargo. Do you know what it is?"

The waiter brought our order and I sat quietly until he left our table. Scotty eyed the server and waited until he was gone. He leaned closer to me and lowered his voice.

"Beta-E is the key ingredient in Crunch Dust. It's what gives the user that euphoric feeling and light-headed sensation when they take the narcotic." Scotty stated dryly. "The beta-blocker in the chemical acts as an opiate and also magnifies the effects of the ephedrine. How did you find out you were carrying this?"

"That mechanic I introduced to you, Doolie. He thought I knew it was part of the cargo and was my primary reason for coming to Nexus. He inadvertently started talking about it."

"So Kurlie set you up to smuggle a chemical used to manufacture a narcotic. What do you want to do?"

"Not much I can do but play along for now. Besides, I need to make sure the Zephyr gets fixed the way I want it. I want departure as soon as possible."

"How soon can they have your ship repaired?"

"Doolie thinks he can have her ready in the next two days. There's a chance we may be able to get out of here by the 28th."

"What are you going to do about Kurlie when we get back to Earth?"

"I don't know yet. I'll figure that out when we get back."

"Okay, Nikki, I'll try to get things wrapped up here in the next day or so. Until then," Scotty nodded, "you stay alert and be careful. Here's my room and phone number at the hotel," He took out a pen, wrote it down on a piece of paper, and slid it to me, "call me if you need anything."

"Thanks." I exhaled as I put his number in my jacket.

Scotty leaned back into his chair, "All of a sudden things are moving fast," he said thoughtfully, "Montrell's connected to someone big in Fluture."

"Yeah, someone named Charon. This was supposed to be my last run, but it seems that people here are expecting me to bring more Beta-E." I frowned. "I have a feeling Kurlie's going to lean on me about deliveries to Nexus."

"The way I see it, Montrell roped you into circumstances that will end badly. If you don't make the runs, your ass is in a sling for knowing too much about their operation." Scotty paused.

"If you continue to work through this, I think you'll eventually end up in the reeds for the same reason." He said grimly as he folded his hands on the table. "You're an expendable asset standing in a puddle of shit, Nikki, and you haven't got the right shoes for it."

"The future doesn't sound too promising, does it?"

"These things don't just work themselves out."

"I know. Can you give me a ride back to the Zephyr? I need to pick up my ride and bring it back here, I'm going back to Fluture tonight."

Chapter 10

That evening, Scott slipped into the parking garage with his backpack and moved the SS-2 to a more secluded location in the corner of the fifth level of the structure that wasn't covered by the security cameras. If the car was bugged, whoever is tracking him would think one of the valets just shuffled the sedan to a different spot.

He sat in the car for about ten minutes and looked around to make sure he was alone, he could hear the echo of engines on the lower levels, but so far no one came up here. After a while, he was satisfied this would be a secure enough place to take care of the task at hand.

He reached down and popped the hood open. Scott got out and scanned the engine for a few minutes then checked the wheel wells and fender. Not having any luck, he began his search inside. Forty minutes later, he found two magnetic tracking devices: one was hidden in the steering column, the other was behind the screen of the Avarno's GPS system. He examined the transmitters and smiled, then pocketed the small instruments and pulled the Black Swan out of the pack with the det-receiver rings.

Scott took the plastic explosive and shaped them onto the engine block. He stopped for a moment to scan the area to make sure he was still unobserved, then plunged the prongs of the detonation rings into the Swan. He shut the hood, sat down in the car, and took the Kirsten automatic pistol out of the backpack with the extra clips and taped them under the dashboard next to the steering column.

He left the SS-2 parked in the corner and walked down two levels of the garage when he was done. There was a luxury sedan parked next to the entrance of the elevator lobby; he strolled up to it, and stuck the locators under the bumper.

Scott showered and put on some casual clothes when he got back to his room on the eighth floor. He put on a black dinner jacket, stepped out to the balcony, and gazed at the lights of Fluture. The streets were bright with the flow of traffic, and the nearby glass highrises mirrored each other as they stretched into the night sky. The sound of the avenue was faint, but he could still hear the music from the clubs rising to his level. Another night in the city of lights.

He caught a movement in the shadows from the corner of his eye. Scott turned his head to the right and saw it; a Blue Didius Butterfly--delicate and beautiful, its wingspan was at least ten inches across. It fluttered gently as it crawled on the handrail opening and closing its wings slowly. Scott smiled as it stopped less than two feet from him, and he watched it fiddle with its legs and clean it's antennae. It was hard to believe such a fragile creature could venture thousands of miles from its birthplace then find its way home. It must be among the first to arrive and he knew that thousands more would be following soon.

He kept his eyes on the Didius as he backed into his room slowly. He spent a few minutes double-checking his things then went down to The Orchid Casino.

The place was packed. Gamblers were a different breed of people; they obsessed over chance and its indifference to the human condition, and even when faced with loss, many couldn't walk away from the table because they felt they could somehow control fate--the counters that tried to tame luck with hard mathematics and statistical voodoo. But for Scott, nothing was left to chance, everything was a calculated move, and luck was a factor in the equation that was reduced as much as possible.

He moved through the crowd watching people playing Black Ball, Lucky 13, Cyber Six, and G-Ride. There was a constant ringing or chiming in the air as machines lit up and monitors gave a live feed of an elimination race going on in another part of Nexus.

He spotted Charon with a couple of bodyguards walking around the tables watching people engrossed in their games. They were looking for hustlers or teams of them that were working the house. So that's Charon. The next time he would see him would be from a distance of twenty-five hundred meters. Tomorrow he would go to the valley and set up.

It was about one in the morning and the darkness held a slight chill as I pushed down on the Cyclone's kickstand and grabbed my clutch bag. This time the valet from the night before had recognized me but still seemed a little embarrassed by his earlier mistake.

"Good evening, Miss."

"Hello." I responded. "Is the Electric Gypsy still open?"

"Yes, as far as I know it should be open for another hour or so. May I take that helmet for you?"

"I'll hang on to it this evening. Have you ever gone in there?"

"I like to go on my nights off."

"Is it the same DJ every night?"

"You mean Herron?"

"Yeah."

"Yes, Herron's the man, he really knows how to work the crowd. The ladies love him."

"Do you know when he usually leaves?"

"I'm afraid any information concerning the staff is privileged." The valet grinned.

166

"I understand." I slipped him a hundred and winked. "This is for taking such good care of my personal belongings last night while I was at the Gypsy."

He sighed, "He gets all the girls. You want to meet him don't you?"

"I find him interesting." I smiled.

The valet glanced at the tip I gave him. "Sheesh, if you go around the east end of the casino, you'll see a door by the loading docks. Go through it and take a right down the corridor, then go left. Herron's dressing room is the second door on the right."

"Thanks."

I walked briskly down the side of the building in the shadows avoiding the parking lot lights, then I heard voices as I got closer to the docks. I slowed my pace, put my back to the wall, and edged closer, until I could peer around the corner of the building.

I saw two men dressed in ERT uniforms carrying a blonde girl to a red Medevac van. I stood quietly in the darkness and listened in on their conversation as they loaded her into the vehicle.

"...so wadda ya think, yhamo?." One of them asked gruffly as he pulled the girl into the van.

"I'll tell ya what I think...I think you and I are in the wrong line of work," the other responded bitterly, "she's the forth one tonight."

"He's definitely running hot, ain't he?"

"Yeah. She's a good specimen though."

They shut the back doors of the vehicle, got in, and drove off into the night. I slipped into the building and walked through the corridor until I found Herron's dressing room. I looked around and was comforted that the late hours left the area uninhabited by staff members.

I tapped on the door lightly and was greeted heatedly by Herron's voice.

"Jase, I told you I'd meet you upstairs in an hour!"

I opened the door and stepped into the dressing room. Herron was sitting in front of a large mirror framed by lights. His stovepipe hat was on the floor, and his face was still painted red and white with make-up. His shirt was off and he looked up at my reflection with surprise.

"Well hello there little lady," he grinned as he turned around and stood up to face me, "I'll assume you came here because you wanted to feast your eyes on the star and maybe go home and tell your friends you pillowed the Gypsy's DJ."

"Not really." I swung my helmet as hard as I could and nailed Herron on the left side of his head. He flew sideways

168

and smashed the mirror with his forehead before his eyes rolled white and he twisted slowly toward me with his mouth agape, then ended up sprawled on the floor face down and out cold.

I picked him up, propped him on his chair facing what was left of the dresser mirror, and tore his shirt into ribbons. I used them to bound his hands behind him and legs to the chair.

I had to work quickly if I was going to pull this off. I needed to keep him off balance by not giving him a chance to think, I had to instill fear and exploit it.

I grabbed a table lamp and pulled the cord out of its base. I noticed that Herron had his nipples pierced and gold loops dangled from each one. Perfect. I split the cord in half, took my knife and stripped about two inches of insulation from the end to expose the wires.

I wrapped each bare wire around Herron's nipple rings, and plugged the cord into the nearest outlet that was circuited to a light switch.

I picked up a bottle of water that sat on his dresser and poured some on his head. Herron inhaled loudly and coughed as he regained consciousness.

"What the hell!" He barked raggedly as he looked at the wires attached to his body. "What are you doing?"

"Hello Herron," I frowned as I crossed my arms and faced him, "you and I need to have a little talk."

"Ha-ha! Piss-off, bitch!" He blurted defiantly.

"Uh-huh." I sighed, leaned forward, and jammed what was left of his shirt into his mouth. "So we do this the hard way."

I took the bottle of water and poured it on his chest as I flicked on the light switch. Herron's body stiffened in the chair and his eyes bulged as he convulsed hard. I turned off the switch after forty-five seconds and pulled the rag out of his mouth.

"Goddamn it!" He huffed as he glared at me.

"You know, I could do this all night." I said calmly as I ran my fingers through his wet hair. "The only problem is that I don't have all night." I grinned as I swirled a tuft of hair with my index finger and stepped behind him.

"What do you want?" Herron growled.

"Answers." I stated dryly, clutched a hand full of hair, and pulled his head back hard so that he looked up at me. "I know you're job at the Gypsy is just a cover for something else. I want to know who you work for and how your operation works."

"You're out of your fooking head...do you know who you're messing with?" Herron laughed.

170

"Last night after midnight a girl disappeared while she was with you. Tonight four more vanished because of you."

"How do you know this?" He gasped. "You a cop?"

I pulled out my knife and pressed it against his right cheek. "After you get a girl geeked-up on crunch, what else do you give them to get them so whacked? Last I heard, crunch was an amphetamine."

"It's mixed with harquinol."

"A super opiate." I nodded. "You dose them with a speed demon."

"Yeah." Herron smiled.

"Where do they get taken when they pass-out?"

"No." He shook his head and looked down as he struggled against his constraints.

"No?" I asked with exaggerated surprise.

"Get stuffed!"

"I'm afraid your answer is unacceptable." I replied and stuffed the rag back into his mouth and hit the switch again. Herron seized-up and I could hear him choke as saliva foamed from the corners of his mouth.

I shut the switch off again and yanked the cloth out. "I'm running out of patience, Herron, and you're running out of time…"

"OH GOD STOP! PLEASE STOP!" He pleaded.

"...what happens to the girls you drug when they get taken out of here?" I asked coldly.

Herron cried. "You don't understand, they're going to kill me if I talk!"

"No, you don't understand--they're not in charge of you right now, I am." I glared. "The only difference is that I'll make you wish you died as a child by the time I'm done."

I showed him my blade again as we looked at his reflection in a jagged shard of mirror. "See this? It's not the ideal tool for what I'm going to do, but still, it'll get the job done." I drew the blade lightly across his cheek and a thin line of blood appeared.

"Jaysus," he cringed, "what are you going to do to me?" Herron's eyes widened.

"My knife is sharp but this is going to get really sloppy when I start cutting." I whispered. "You see, the layer of dermis has a lot of nerves in it, so when I start to flay your face, you're going to feel it separate from the connective tissue beneath." I smiled sadistically. I had to push my bluff, get him to believe that I drew pleasure from what I was doing...

"The muscles on the face are intricate...a beautiful matrix, really. We're going to have ourselves an anatomy lesson, and when I'm done, I'm going to stick your face on the wall so you can see the expression you had when I peeled it off your skull."

"I'LL TALK! I'LL TALK! PLEASE, NO MORE!" He begged.

"Where do they go when they leave here?"

"They get taken to Cybelle."

"What happens there?"

"Charon breaks them down and uses them as call girls at The Orchid. Sometimes he sells them off to the high bidders in a place called The Chamber."

"What do you mean he breaks them down?"

"He keeps 'em doped, has one of his guys threaten and beat them, whatever it takes to break their spirit into submission."

"Where's this Chamber?"

"Cybelle."

"You've been to this chamber?"

"Only once."

"So you kidnap girls for a prostitution and sex slave ring."

Herron didn't answer. He slouched and looked down at the floor shaking his head.

"Where do you keep your stash of crunch?" I demanded.

"What? Why?"

"I'm asking the questions around here! Now where do you keep your shit?"

"Top..." Herron motioned to the dresser. "...top drawer."

I sheathed my knife, opened the drawer and found a half-filled bag of white powder. I dumped its contents into a pile on the dresser, pulled out the Cobalt, and put it against Herron's right temple.

"What are you going to do?" He asked as he regarded the pile of crunch.

"It's party time." I grabbed the hair on the top of his head and forced him down toward the dust.

"NO! NO!" He cried pathetically as I pushed his face into the pile.

"Breeaaathe!" I said through clenched teeth.

"Mmmrrrffttt!" Herron struggled as I buried his face in the narcotic.

His body went limp after a few seconds, and I pulled his head up. Crunch was smeared all over his face and his pupils were dilated and glassy. Herron's mouth hung open and he began to drool on himself.

I put the Cobalt away, flicked the switch back on, and left him convulsing in the room.

Summer mindlessly pushed the food around on her plate as she stared at the glass of wine in front of her. She paid no mind to the background conversations of the other patrons of the restaurant as she lost herself in thought. She was tired and just wanted to get back to her room.

The man she was escorting this evening was a very ~~PLATINUM~~ distinguished executive for one of the largest ~~plutonium~~ mining companies in Nexus. He was in his late sixties, balding, overweight, and rich. One of her regulars.

One thing clients like him had in common was that they were all married, had families, and used their business trips to cheat on their wives. Money seemed to be no object for them to have their fantasies fulfilled...no matter how depraved. She was their girl. The girl that never flinched. The girl that never judged.

You'd never know it by looking at him, but this one was kind of a freak; that was always the case with his kind, straight-laced and conservative in appearance, with a dark unsettling fetish lurking behind an expensive suit.

He always tipped her a lot of money on the side to "be treated extra special." Extra special meant that he would snort some crunch, have her tie him up face down on the floor, and have his ass spanked until it was raw and tears streamed down his face.

He liked to beg, and always insisted she wore spiked heels so she could dig them into his buttocks and tell him what a naughty little boy he was and how he needed to be punished for his impure thoughts.

"You look ravishing tonight, Summer." He smiled as he sipped his wine.

"Thank you, Eli." She blushed.

"I've been looking forward to seeing you again."

"So have I."

"I really enjoyed our last meeting." He grinned. "I can't wait to get you alone."

"Patience. I promise it will be worth the wait."

After they finished their dinner, they retired to his room on the thirteenth floor and he removed his dinner jacket and sat at on the bed.

"Did you bring desert?" Eli asked happily with a tone of anticipation in his voice.

Summer handed him a small vile filled with crunch. He smiled as he unscrewed the cap that had a tiny spoon built into it, took a scoop of the powder, and inhaled it sharply into his left nostril.

"Ahhh! Quality!" He snorted another dip of dust and exhaled loudly as he stood up and completely undressed.

"Oh baby, you *are* a scorcher tonight." He caressed Summer lovingly with his eyes as he fondled himself.

"I've been *really* bad and I think you need to do something extra special to me!"

Summer took a step closer to him and slapped his face hard. "I saw the way you looked at our waitress during dinner and I could tell you were having those dirty thoughts."

"No. I didn't mean it." He pouted as he cast his gaze down at the floor.

"Hey, look at me when I talk to you!" Summer hissed. "You were having thoughts, you dirty little chubby!" She scowled and smacked him again.

"You know what happens when you have those thoughts, right?" Summer said menacingly as she circled him slowly.

"I couldn't help myself!" Eli whined shamefully.

Summer pushed him down to the floor. "On your knees, pizzle! Who do you adore?"

"You."

"Say my name, piglicker!"

"Mistress!"

"Get on your stomach...NOW!

"Yes Empress." The man rolled over submissively.

Summer stood over him and tied his hands behind his back with his neck tie as he sprawled on the carpet. She grabbed the man's belt, folded it in half, and gave his ass five or six hard lashings.

"Oh god!" He yelled. "Harder! Punish me, Mistress!"

"Shut up, you pathetic ass goblin!" Summer ordered as she crossed the belt on Eli's buttocks a few more times with everything she had. His skin was red, and the belt left sharp welts. Tears ran down his cheeks as he took deep breaths and trembled.

"I swear, your ass is hairy enough to pass for a throw rug," Summer's nose crinkled with disgust, "and it smells like burnt mushrooms, you filthy scrub!"

"Oh yes! YES! I'M SO DIRTY!"

"You need to use cream rinse!" Summer whipped him several more times.

"I need cream rinse." He whimpered feebly.

"I want to hear you beg!" She charged as she leaned over him. "What do you want from your Mistress tonight?"

"Pudding."

"What?" Summer growled as she leaned in closer. "I didn't hear you, piglet!"

178

"I want some pudding, my Empress!"

"You have to earn your pudding, you grubby little twat hammer."

"Command me, Mistress."

"I want to hear you sing." She stood up above the man and pressed the stiletto heel of her left shoe into his buttocks as she balanced herself on her right foot. "Sing me my song you shitheel."

"I'm a little teapot, short and stout, here is my handle, here is my spout..." his voice shook with pain...

"With feeling, you miserable knob-gobbler!" Summer put her weight into her left leg and dug the heel of her shoe into his ass cheek...

"Oooh my god that hurts!" He cried loudly.

"Sing dickweed!"

"...when I get all steamed up, hear me shout, tip me up and pour me out..."

"I said with feeling!" Summer removed her foot and began wailing on his ass with the belt with all her might...

"...I'm a clever teapot, yes, it's true..."

"MAGGOT!" She continued to crucify his butt as his voice weakened and sweat poured from him...

"...here's an example of what I can do..."

"LOUDER! Bitch!" She screamed as the belt smacked loudly against his skin and sweat flew in every direction...

"...I can turn my handle into a spout...I want my mommy!"

"Stop crying, bitch!" Summer whipped his ass harder then stood up and jammed her heel into his butt again with her full weight behind it...

"...tip—me—up—and—pour—me--ouuut! MOMMY! I WANT MY MOMMY!" He blubbered in agony.

"What are you?"

"I'm a filthy mud-bunny." He whimpered.

"WRONG!" Summer shouted. "You are a bag of shit!" She slammed her heel into his ass and twisted her foot.

He moaned with his eyes half-closed in ecstasy and passed-out on the floor. Summer took a deep breath, bent down and untied him, and stepped away from Eli's sweaty body.

She calmly walked to the dresser and took a moment to fix her hair. Summer glanced up at the reflection of the man as she touched-up her lipstick.

She went over to the bed and picked up Eli's pants and pulled his billfold out of the back pocket. Summer counted out four thousand credits, put it in her purse, and left the room.

Chapter 11

Kurlie

Larron and Vince looked exhausted when they came to see me. I could tell from their glassy-eyed expressions that they hadn't slept in days, but Vince looked excited as he walked into the room, sat next to Larron, and set three burned-out SCaT pads on my desk.

Hackers. I don't know what it is about them, but they all seemed the same: rogue brainiacs that got their ya-ya's off on sleep deprivation as they tested network security codes and exposed the vulnerabilities of mega-corporations by deciphering and dissecting their firewalls, hijacking identities, and disrupting the flow of daily life, and for what? A jab at the establishment? To bring chaos into the lives of people by reminding them that no matter how safe they thought they were someone was always around to put the hoodoo into their existence? Odd people.

"So, have you made any progress with Scott's identity?" I asked optimistically.

"Here's the story Mr. Montrell," Vince replied apprehensively, "every time Larron and I tried to get the goods on Scott we hit a wall. We think his profile is phony, someone's gone through a lot of trouble to make-up certs for this guy."

"The man doesn't exist...well no shit. What the hell am I paying you for? Tell me something I don't know."

"Oh he exists all right, just not in the way you and I exist. When you told us how Tommy was killed, Larron and I suspected that any information dragnet on a Fenmore Scott would trigger a trackware that would backwash the probing system." Vince pointed at the damaged SCaT pads. "As you can see, we tested the theory and some hardware got smoked."

"So instead of trying to find something out about Scott's past," Larron interceded, "we decided to look at what was going in and out of Nexus, we hoped we could pick up some leads."

"Ship manifests for the corporations importing goods to the planet were easy to harvest." Vince smiled.

"We didn't find anything useful there," Larron continued, "so we focused on the blackmarket for anything out of the ordinary; we found drugs and weapons...basically the kind of contraband you'd expect to be brought into a planet that's still being developed."

"Then I found a small encrypted packing list for a cargo drop that was made in Northern Icarus." Vince said excitedly.

"It took us a day to crack the script but we finally managed to decode it." Larron cut in. "Everything on the list is impossible to get on the street, so someone paid a fortune to get these items."

"Talk to me guys."

"Black Swan with imploder rings and a transmitter."

"What's Black Swan?"

"It's a plastic explosive used exclusively by the Terekian military. You have to have connections to get this kind of tear-ass swag and the device it takes to detonate it. An ounce of Swan can level a city block and leave a thirty-foot deep crater in the ground."

"What else?"

Larron and Vince looked at each other quietly.

"What else did you find on that list, goddamn it!"

"A Kirsten Automatic assault pistol, and armor-piercing hollow point rounds. All this was purchased in Fluture last month."

"Shit! Any idea who made the buy?"

"No sir. We looked into it, but it was a dead end."

"I'm being played as a pawn." I slammed my fist on the desktop and made the hackers jump. "If he's there to take someone out, I don't want to be implicated. The last thing I want is to have law enforcement on my ass for landing him in Fluture."

"Anything else we can do, Mr. Montrell?" Vince asked.

"I want you boys to break-off your search and lay low here for the rest of the week, all you're doing is bringing the heat on us when you try to pinpoint this moolie." I turned to look for one of my bodyguards. "Egone, where are you?"

"Yes boss?"

"Get a hold of Max at Gateway and find out when Nikki's supposed to get back to Earth."

"You got it, boss."

"Listen to me, Egone," I said harshly, "the moment Nikki touches down, I need you and six guys to be waiting at the Inter-port to take out Scott."

"We'll be ready for him, Mr. Montrell."

"No room for mistakes, understand? Don't underestimate this bastard. I want you to take him by surprise and I don't want Nikki hurt, either, get it?"

"I'll handle it, boss."

"Whatever his business is in Fluture, I don't want to know about it. As far as I'm concerned, he's Nexus' problem. I could give a damn whether or not he makes it back to Earth. I'm done with this son-of-a-bitch, and I want him dead..."

I jogged down the corridor and made my exit at the side of the building. I slowed to a brisk walk as I approached the lobby of The Orchid.

I noticed a shift change with the valets, and the one that had greeted me was gone for the night. Even at this hour, the place had people lounging around and clients flowed evenly in and out of the casino.

I could cross Herron off the list, now I had to figure out how to get to Charon...I take him out of the picture, then Kurlie's tie to Nexus is broken.

I reached for my SCaT pad and was going to call Scotty when someone tapped me on the shoulder from behind.

"Excuse me, Miss..." An older man in a dark suit smiled.

I felt a sharp sting in my left arm and turned around to see that another man had snuck up on me. "Ouch! What was ththaat?" I slurred as I felt my legs slip away from under me. I felt a surge of warmth wash over my body and my vision blurred before everything darkened and I blacked-out.

When I came to, I found myself in a dim room; my head throbbed with a dull pain, and it was hard to get my eyes to focus on anything. The muscles in my arms were numb and my body felt like lead.

It took me a minute to realize that my hands were bound over my head and I was suspended from a heavy chain that was looped around a huge hydronic pipe main. My feet dangled about a foot off the grated floor.

"Wake up!" A male voice echoed.

I looked up slowly and saw a blurry figure standing in front of me. I wondered how long this drug induced stupor would keep me in a haze.

"Damn it!" Another voice cussed and I felt his hand pull my left eyelid up to examine my state. "Sheesh! I told you not to use too much juice. She's high."

"Back-off, yhamo, I didn't give her the full cocktail."

"She's dorked-out!"

I heard a small snap and coughed as an ammonia capsule was passed under my nose.

"About time you woke up."

"Where am I? What are you doing to me?" I asked as I looked around. The two men from the lobby stood grimly in front of me.

"Let's start with the basics. Who are you, young lady?" The older one demanded.

"Wells. Nikki Wells."

"What are you doing in Fluture?"

"I'm on vacation."

"Vacation?" The man asked sarcastically as he held up my Cobalt. "I'm going to ask you again, what are you doing in Fluture?"

"I got lost on the way to college."

"Have it your way." The older man stepped back and nodded at his partner.

The younger man in the suit stepped forward and punched me in the stomach three times. I tried to clench my teeth but the wind was knocked out of me with every blow, and I swayed backwards from the impact. I coughed hoarsely and gasped for air as stars danced in front of my eyes.

"An hour ago we found a coworker of ours in his dressing room," the older man glowered, "he was doped on crunch and harquinol, and somebody hooked his scrawny ass to a light socket for a massage. Do you know what I'm talking about?"

The man reached up and slapped my face. "Before he died, he managed to tell us about some psycho-groupie bitch that tortured him. As luck would have it, our surveillance cameras caught you leaving his room." He sighed and continued. "What we want to know is how much Herron told you. Tell us that, and we put an end to your pain."

"The only thing I know," I muttered weakly as I looked up at him and tried to catch my breath, "is that your receding hairline…really calls attention to your one eyebrow." I coughed. "You should consider having crop rotation done on your forehead."

The older man smiled and shook his head as he looked at his partner. "Such a waste. I've lost patience with this one." He took out my knife and held it in front of me.

"This look familiar?" He grinned. "Herron said you were going to carve him up with it. I like to play games too, sunshine." He turned the blade slowly in front of me. "I'm going to ask you one more time, if you don't tell me what I need to know, I'm going to start cutting off parts of you. Do we understand each other?"

"Herron told me about..Cybelle…" I whispered faintly as I lowered my head and looked at the floor.

"Come again?" The man tilted his head.

"…Cybelle…"

He took a step toward me as I pulled myself up the chain and kicked his face. The man dropped my knife as he landed on his ass and blood gushed out of his broken nose. His partner pulled out a pistol and pointed it at my head…

"ENOUGH!" A voice boomed from the entrance of the room. "What the hell are you two doing?"

It was Jase. He strode in angrily, glared at my captors, then looked at me.

"IDIOTS!" He barked. "Get her down from there!"

"Mr. Jase," the younger one spoke nervously, "this person is responsible for Herron's death…"

"I said get her down!"

The older man reached up and untied me while his cohort gently lowered me to the floor.

"Mr. Jase, she may be jeopardizing the operation."

"She's part of the operation, you fucking imbecile." Jase crouched down and dabbed the beads of perspiration from my face with a handkerchief. "What happened to your face, Asoy?"

"Bah! Who is she, Mr. Jase?"

"Someone more important than you." Jase said coolly as he stood up, pulled a pistol with a sound suppressor out of his jacket, and shot the older man in the head.

His startled partner backed up in fear as he instinctively held his hands in front of his face, "NO! Please…"

Jase pointed his pistol at the man's head and pulled the trigger. He paused for a second, then stepped over to me and carefully helped me to my feet. "Can you walk? Come on, we don't have much time, let's get you back to Cybelle."

My vision blurred as I stood up, then everything around me went hazy and I passed out.

Scott drove the SS-2 up the winding two-lane street that ascended the eastern ridge of Sertina Valley. The road was lined heavily with tall birch-like trees on both sides and the flora was thick and green along the shoulders.

He drove with the window down and could smell the sweet fragrance of the flowering plants that flourished in these mountains as the cool air brushed against his face.

The Avarno was definitely designed for performance and cornered extremely well on the hairpin turns. It was fast and luxurious; a vehicle that fit in with the high-end communities established in the valley.

He took note of the sparse traffic and slowed down after another car traveling the opposite direction passed him and disappeared from site in his rearview mirror.

Scott pulled off the street onto a dirt path that cut through the forest. The trail narrowed and the terrain got rougher as he drove further away from the main road. He kept his speed down to avoid kicking-up too much dust as he drove another ten minutes on the isolated pathway.

He checked the car's GPS and came to a stop. This was it. It had to be. Scott pulled over to the side and backed the car into a copse of trees and brush. He checked his watch and waited an hour as he scanned his surroundings and memorized the lay of the land.

It was late afternoon and he watched the shadows shift on the ground as the minutes ticked away. Scott closed his eyes and slowed his breathing as he cleared his mind. He didn't think about the mission or what he had to do to carry it out.

There was a part of himself deep inside that he had to find and reconnect with; a part that he had not seen in a long time--a part of another existence when survival was grounded on instinct and cunning, and his actions instilled fear in his prey: the fear of looking over your shoulder for someone who wasn't there, the fear of being hunted by a predator that had no mercy...

...he felt himself slip into the fragmented memories of his broken past: a warrior lying motionless in the forest--host to the chill brought by a winter rain the night before, wet leaves against his face as a ground fog eddied lifelessly around him...the cold, indifferent shades of a grey dawn creeping across the ground...a dirty face illuminated by fires leaping against the dark sky as he watched shadows dance through a scope...the crack of high-powered rifles shattering the silence of first light...the split-second expression of release on his adversary's face as a cloud of red filled the air...the thick, coppery smell of blood, and the silence of the aftermath. Scott opened his eyes and saw the translucent reflection of his face on the windshield. His eyes were cold and dead. He had resurrected the assassin.

Scott got out of the car and opened the trunk. He looked over the gear he had prepared, took out the ghillie suit, and put it on. He made a few adjustments before he pulled the hood over his head and slipped on his gloves.

He reached down and opened the flat case that contained the parts of the M341 and assembled the Trinity in under a minute. He took the rifle's twelve-round magazine and inserted the four explosive rounds first, the two armor-piercing hollow points were next, then he took a single round out of his pocket and looked at it.

It was the one projectile that made the journey with him from Earth. A Halon & Wood two-staged tungsten jacketed hollow point. Flat black with the manufacturers name in yellow lettering stamped into its casing, Scott turned the bullet slowly between his index finger and thumb as he examined it with reverence, he slid it into the clip, and slapped the mag deftly into the rifle. It was time.

Scott took a few steps back from the car, turned to scan the thickets around him, then vanished silently into the forest.

He moved through the thick brush and vines quietly as he made his way through the woods. He paid special attention to the landscape and made sure he didn't leave a trail of broken branches or footprints in the bed of leaves and pine needles as he cut his own path.

He listened to the chirps and buzzes of birds and insects that surrounded him. Except for the occasional whoop of squirrel monkeys, he was alone and could hear the beat of his own heart as he walked with the M341 held at port. Scott stopped every few minutes just to listen and keep his senses connected with the environment.

The trees here were bunched close together and their foliage kept it cool in the dimming valley. He had another quarter of a mile before he got to the place he selected as the location to view the strike point.

Scott glanced at the GPS watch just to get his bearings and make sure he was moving in the right direction. It was getting darker and he wanted to be in position by nightfall to get the Trinity dialed in.

He could hear the rustle of leaves overhead as a breeze came from the west. He looked up and saw a large group of monkeys skipping noisily through the branches above him. Sertina Valley was still an untapped wilderness rich with wildlife. The communities built on the sides of the mountains displaced many species, but the majority of the valley remained an untouched sanctuary.

The ground had a gradual slope and Scott could see some of the posh country houses on the opposite side of the valley. There weren't a lot of homes on the face of the mountain, but the ones that were built were mansions seated in acres of vineyards growing on shelves carved into the face of the massif.

Then he saw it, Charon's villa. A white, two story structure cut into the eastern face of the valley surrounded by towering trees covered with thick moss. There were wide marble steps that descended to a circular driveway on the south end of the property where a large fountain was centered. He shouldered the Trinity as he dropped to a knee, took out a range finder, and scanned parts of the villa to get his distance established.

This was a good vantage point; it was slightly elevated from the villa and the vegetation was lush and impenetrable with the naked eye. From his position, Scott could clearly see the master bedroom on the second level and most of the courtyard that led to the driveway. The main entryway was obscured by the thick ivy that grew on the east walls and draped over the lower patios. He was a little over two thousand meters away.

About forty yards in front of him was a sheer drop of sixty meters into the jagged banks of a wide river that flowed between the mountain ridges. Scott went prone in the bushes where he could see the villa between the trunks of two Allura pines and over the tops of the trees in the valley below.

It was getting dark and he was tired. Scott unfolded a bi-pod with spiked feet and attached it to the barrel of the Trinity before positioning it on the hard ground in front of him. He removed the lens covers for the scope and began making his adjustments on the kill zone. He planned on taking the shot tomorrow morning, but first, he had to wait for him to arrive.

The weather forecast for tomorrow was clear and sunny, and there was an eight mile an hour wind from the north.

The temperature was supposed to be eleven degrees Celsius as the low, so he would allow for that as a minor variable to be worked into the equation for bullet-drop and flight time in the distance between him and Charon.

Scott turned a small knob on the side of the scope to fine-tune the windage, but final changes would have to be done in the morning.

Charon was a creature of habit like many people. He was predictable and his routines were easy to memorize. Scott spent weeks studying him, and even knew about his preference for certain brands of wine and the days he like to drink them. He knew that Charon considered the villa his real home as opposed to his apartment in the city, and he always came here midweek to roost and to get away from the crowds of Fluture. But he always returned to the casino on Saturday night when things were in full swing.

The valley began to quiet down as darkness slowly set in. It was 1900 hours and Scott could see the silhouette of the ridge against the night sky. The stars filled the heavens but he peered through the scope at the villa observing the staff moving about the property.

There was one security guard, a cook, and the maid. A decorative wroth iron gate covered with cat's claw vines ran around the property's perimeter, and most of the lights in the mansion were on. They were expecting Charon tonight.

He scanned the second floor and noted the wide terrace for the master bedroom. There was a bistro set on the balcony and ivy clung stubbornly on the stone handrails. He noted two sliding glass doors that led to the master suite, and the vertical blinds were left open for the evening. He could see the round king size bed positioned close to the north wall of the room, and the door that led to the bathroom.

Scott's breathing was quiet as he put the crosshairs on the bodyguard's head. Two thousand and three meters. He clicked the variable magnification function on the Trinity's scope to thirty times and traced the guard's movement in the garden. He was heading toward the driveway.

Three black cars pulled up in a line to the steps and stopped; the center car was a limousine, and the lead and last cars were sedans. Charon stepped out of the limo with a young brunette wearing a black evening gown, and two well-dressed body guards stepped out of each sedan. Scott could tell from the slight bulge in the men's jackets that they were all armed, possibly with compact automatic weapons.

Charon put his arm around the girl as they ascended into the villa while his security team stayed in the courtyard. He had a hell of an entourage, counting his drivers, there were eight men on his security team.

Scott took a deep breath and continued to study the strike point. Charon's lifestyle was one of excess and was funded by mercilessly victimizing anyone that crossed his path.

Tomorrow it would end. Tomorrow he would die...

I opened my eyes and found myself back in my room in Cybelle. My whole body hurt and I was disoriented as I turned my head and looked around trying to focus.

"Jase, she's awake!" I heard a female voice call excitedly and felt a cold wash cloth placed on my forehead as a shadow loomed over me.

"What..."

"Shhh, Nikki, take it easy, you're safe now." The voice said reassuringly as she dabbed by face with the wash cloth.

I was able to make out the face hovering over me as my vision cleared. It was Summer. "Summer? What are you doing here? How did I get here?"

"Jase brought us both here." She smiled shyly.

"Hello Ms. Wells." Jase said calmly as he walked over and stood next to Summer. "How are you feeling?"

"I've had better days." I grimaced as I sat up and put a hand over my stomach. "Damn that hurts! I remember now," I frowned, "thanks for your help, Jase."

"I'm sorry I didn't get to you sooner, Ms. Wells," Jase said apologetically, "I didn't know until the last minute that those two had taken you into custody."

"Don't worry about it. How long have I been out?"

"Two hours." Jase said as he draped a blanket on my shoulders.

"What time is it?"

"Quarter to five."

"I need to start packing."

"We already took care of that for you." Summer nodded. "You need to rest."

"She's right Ms. Wells," Jase cleared his throat, "yesterday was a long day for you. You need to rest up for your trip home."

"You still haven't answered my question Summer, what are you doing here?" I pressed.

"Ms. Wells," Jase interrupted, "we need a huge favor," he paused, "I need you to take Summer back to Earth with you when you leave today."

I squinted at Summer, and her expression looked worried. I turned and looked at Jase. "Is my ship ready?"

"It will be fueled in a few hours. I think Doolie and his men did a great job on the repairs. They managed to get the Zephyr space worthy a day ahead of schedule."

"Why are you helping me?" I asked suspiciously. "One thing I've learned over the years in my line of work is that everyone has an angle--everyone's got a story. Tell me why you're so willing to help. Aren't you Charon's right-hand man?

This evening I saw you execute two men without flinching, and now you just expect me to take you at your word? I don't believe good samaritans exist, Jase. What's your angle? What's in it for you?"

"I don't expect you to trust me, Ms. Wells," Jase sighed, "but I have my reasons."

Summer reached over and tenderly took Jase's hand into her own. Her eyes were welling with tears. Jase paused for a few seconds and looked at her. He nodded as he patted her hand the way a father would comfort his own child.

"I'm not a Terran like you and Summer, I'm half Serenian and my father was Tyberian. Do you know what that means, Ms. Wells?" Jase looked at me distantly.

"Enlighten me, Jase." I crossed my arms.

"My lifespan is roughly half of yours, Ms. Wells. I'm forty-nine years old; I've got one year left and that will be my end."

Jase let go of Summer's hand and sat down next to me. "I've seen and done a lot of terrible things over the years," Jase reflected, "I have many regrets. Maybe I just want to do one good thing before I'm done...perhaps making a difference in someone's life can offset some of the dreadful things I've done.

Summer is a good person, Ms. Wells. She deserves more than what Nexus has to offer. If I can make a difference in her life, then maybe my own hasn't been a total waste and something good came from my existence. If I never do anything right again, at least I'll have done this." Jase looked at me pleadingly, "Please Ms. Wells, I beg of you, take Summer with you."

"Please Nikki," Summer said softly, "I won't be any trouble. I just have to get out of Fluture. Jase did save you and he's the reason your ship was repaired so quickly."

"What about my partner Scotty?" I asked. "You know I'm not leaving until he gets back here."

"I wouldn't worry about him, Ms. Wells, as far as Charon is concerned, you and Mr. Scott are about to become his new pipeline from Earth. Can you get him back here this morning?"

"We've already made arrangements."

"So you'll bring Summer?"

"How soon can you have my ship online?"

"I can promise you'll be sitting in the flight deck by 0900 hours."

"Then you've got a deal." I reached out my hand and Jase smiled as he shook it. "Please tell Doolie I want to start my preflight in three hours."

"I am in your debt, Ms. Wells."

I looked at Summer. "Have you ever done space travel, Summer?"

"No, this is a first for me." She replied meekly.

"You're packed? You have everything you need?"

"Yes. I believe so."

"I've taken the liberty of getting you an Inter-port identification pass." Jase said softly to Summer as he handed her the passport card.

"She'll need a flight suit." I said as I stood up and checked my personal things.

"Done. I'll talk to Doolie about getting one for her." Jase stated. "If you two will excuse me, I have other matters to tend to before your departure." Jase said grimly as he stood up and walked out.

I sat quietly for a few seconds. "Can he be trusted, Summer?"

"He's the only real friend I have in Fluture."

Chapter 12

Axium and Allure, Nexus' two moons, were full and cast their pale light over the landscape, silvering the trees and charging the darkness with life. They seemed to call out to the inhabitants of the forest and bring out the savageness of the alien night.

Scott lay motionless as he listened to the sound of predator footsteps around him, he could hear the baying of Northern Tavara Böri packs that echoed through the valley followed by the shrieks of animals that fell prey to them.

He found a peculiar comfort in his environment, it was as if he belonged here; deep in the forest amidst the sweet aroma of genesis and decay, the bloom of Icra orchids, and the cold dampness of the thick moss--alone and as gray as the creatures that roamed the woods.

He felt at one with the darkness--the host that embraced him and revealed its eerie secrets; the ghostly silhouettes that moved silently in the chill, the whisper of featherless wings flapping in the gloom, and the Icarus birches and pines that towered around him. Guardians that kept silent time of unseen change.

The hours waned as Scott watched the moons trek across the valley. Eventually, the thin blue line of dawn appeared on the horizon, faint and wintery. First light slowly reached for the heavens and shaded the land as a light fog drifted lifelessly over the moist ground and a surreal stillness filled the morning air.

The valley had turned blue, a dreamlike hue in the mists. During the night, thousands of Didius butterflies had descended into the area. They were everywhere, Didius covered everything and their wings opened and closed slowly like blooming flowers as they clung to every tree and leaf in the valley. It was a breathtaking sight, and Scott was astonished by their numbers and exquisiteness as he stared at the mountainside--spellbound by the beauty of the event.

He snapped out of his gaze and peered through the Trinity's scope at the villa. In the minutes he allowed himself to be distracted, someone had drawn open the blinds for the sliding glass doors of Charon's bedroom, and he could see the young girl curled in a heap of silk sheets, but Charon was nowhere in sight. Three bodyguards were in the driveway loitering around the limo, but he couldn't see anyone else in the estate.

Then he appeared. Wearing a plush white bathrobe, Charon stepped out onto the terrace holding a cup of coffee. He moved casually toward the bistro set, put his mug on the table, and stretched his arms over his head and yawned as he leaned on the rail and looked at the butterflies in the valley.

Scott put the crosshairs between Charon's eyes; his breathing was slow and shallow as he wrapped his index finger around the trigger. He turned a small, horizontal knob on the scope to adjust the windage one more time.

Scott checked his range. Two thousand and ten meters. He turned a vertical knob on the scope slowly, and put the crosshairs just to the left and slightly higher than Charon's head...

Scott blinked slowly and brought his breathing under control as he watched Charon taking in the magnificence of daybreak...

...I am become death...

...he exhaled and squeezed the trigger smoothly. The Trinity bumped his shoulder lightly as a muffled pop broke the silence and the casing ejected...

He watched through the scope as Charon's head blew apart in a cloud of blood, his fractured body violently twisted clockwise and fell onto the patio...

Scott could see the deck darken with blood as Charon twitched involuntarily. He saw the girl sit up on the bed and turn her head toward the balcony, her mouth was open in a scream as she put her hands to her face in terror.

The double doors for the master suite suddenly slammed open as two guards rushed into room with their weapons drawn to see what was going on...

Scott squinted and squeezed the trigger of the M341 twice. The first man into he bedroom took the round in the face;

the back of his head blew open and his body was thrown backwards from the impact as the round traveled through and splintered the door they just came through.

The second guard fell to his knees as he clutched his throat and blood gushed between his fingers. He staggered on his hands and knees for a few seconds before he fell face down on the floor. The girl jumped out of the bed and wrapped a sheet around herself as she continued to scream hysterically at the bodies that surrounded her.

The men in the driveway turned their heads toward the commotion in the villa and pulled out their firearms...

Scott aimed at the limo's engine block and fired another round. The car exploded in a ball of fire that engulfed the men as they were thrown to the ground by the blast. The limo smoldered in flames as black smoke rose into the air. The dead guards were sprawled on the pavers among the smoking debris, and one of them was on fire.

The explosion resonated through the valley and the butterflies erupted into flight and filled the sky. The sound of birds flared up as the mountainside came to life with the chatter of animals.

One of the drivers ran out to driveway and saw the chaos, he quickly turned around and ran back into the villa in a panic. Scott could see the mayhem and confusion in the mansion as the staff stumbled around in the living room. He figured Charon's drivers were trained security professionals like the guards, but Scott could tell by their reaction that they weren't. They were just as confused and frightened as the maid and cook.

Still, he couldn't afford to take any chances. He fired two more shots and the sedans blew up and sent twisted panels cartwheeling across the driveway. He watched the people in the villa jump from the sound of the explosions and take cover behind the furniture. He had put the fear in them and was satisfied that they would be paralyzed by it.

He got up and folded the bipod of the rifle. Scott knew he was on borrowed time and had to make it back to Cybelle as fast as possible. It was now 0630 hours and he didn't have much time. He shouldered the Trinity and started to run through the woods back to the Avarno.

He knew calls would be made and tried to anticipate how the dynamics of his situation would be changed. He would adopt and improvise. He was on pure instinct now.

His breathing was steady as he zigzagged through the trees and ducked low branches. The ground was soft and spongy from the bed of pine needles and leaves, and with every step he ran, butterflies took flight from their resting place and insects leapt from the forest floor.

After the blasts, Scott figured he had fifteen minutes--twenty tops, before law enforcement arrived at the scene and began throwing up roadblocks for at least a twenty-mile radius. He was also anticipating aerial drones to swarm the valley in a sweep. He had to move fast. He only had a half mile run to the car, but getting back to Cybelle undetected was another obstacle to overcome. He hoped Nikki and the Zephyr would be ready.

He heard barking and howling as he jumped over a rotted log covered with black moss. He glanced to his right and saw the blur of black stripes and gray fur of four Tavara Böri chasing him as he sprinted through the woods. He was being hunted like an animal by the mammals. Tavara were fast and very aggressive pack hunters; they were sleek, weighed in at eighty to ninety pounds, and had six legs. There was no way he was going to out run them.

Scott pulled out the Raven, slowed his pace, and squeezed off two rounds. One of the Tavara yelped as it fell to the ground, and the other three scattered into the bushes. He started running again when he heard the brush in front of him part as one of the creatures leapt in the air and hit him hard enough to send him flying backwards.

He slammed onto the ground and his pistol was knocked out of his hand as the Tavara got on top and bared its fangs with a growl. Scott instinctively grabbed it by the throat with his left hand to keep its snapping jaws away from his face. The beast was strong and he could feel its full weight on him as it lunged forward. He struggled wildly and could feel the Tavara's claws digging painfully into his abdomen. He saw the Raven on the ground a few feet away to his right, but it was out of reach.

The Tavara broke loose from his grip and managed to sink its teeth into his left forearm and shake it's head. He screamed in agony from the pressure of the bite as its fangs gouged deep lacerations into his flesh. His only saving grace was that it was his bio-mech arm, otherwise the Tavara would have broken it.

He pulled his legs up between him and the Tavara in a fetal-like position and kicked the beast off him. Scott rolled to his right as the Tavara landed on its back; he grabbed the Raven and fired from a kneeling position as the Tavara lunged at him again. The animal was instantly killed in mid-air but still crashed into him with enough force to leave him sprawled on the ground.

Scott got back on his feet and started running. He could feel the throb of the creature's bite on his forearm and he was bleeding badly. Even though his arm was biomechanical, he could still feel the immense pain from the wound. His abdomen was also bleeding.

He staggered the last few yards to the car and ripped off the ghillie suit as he opened the door and dropped the ghillie and Trinity on the passenger's seat. Scott popped the trunk open, grabbed the backpack, and set it next to him in the cab. He tore a strip off the ghillie and wrapped it tightly over his forearm several times to stop the blood flow. It wasn't much, but it would have to do for now.

He fired-up the SS-2, pulled back onto the dirt path and headed for the main road. He was a mess. Time was running out. He looked at the GPS and punched in Cybelle's location as he drove over the bumpy terrain. The mining colony was only twenty-five miles away from his location and the road from these mountains tied into the route that led there.

When he got to the main street he put the hammer down and the trees went by in a green blur as he sped through the winding ridge. It wouldn't take officials long to figure out the trajectory of the shots and start their hunt on the mountainside he left behind.

He made a left when he came to a fork in the road at the bottom of the mountain and merged into the thoroughfare that led straight to Cybelle. The four lane motorway with a center median was a wide, flat run, and unlike the street on the ridge, there were no trees on either side. He was completely exposed…

Jase was in the hanger talking to Doolie when his phone rang.

"Yes?"

It was one of Charon's henchmen in Fluture. He spoke rapidly with an angry tone.

"What? This must be some kind of mistake." Jase frowned as he turned his back to Doolie. "When did this happen? Are you absolutely sure it was Mr. Charon?" He demanded.

"Okay, calm down, Migs," Jase said firmly, "the cops are probably crawling all over the estate and casino right now. I need you to get everyone over here as soon as possible. We need a sit down to figure out who did this and how we're going to deal with them. I want every district boss here in Hanger-6 within the next half hour, understand? Okay, Migs, thank you."

Jase sighed as he put his phone away.

"Everything alright, Mr. Jase?" Doolie asked.

"Charon's been killed." Jase said gravely. "Doolie, get this ship fueled and ready to go--now."

"Yes sir." Doolie looked physically shaken by the news of Charon's demise.

"I'm going to double-up on security for the lab. We're going to have a lot of people here, and I want this freighter out. Tow it if you have to, we're going to need the room. I'll have Demra set up some tables."

Jase grabbed the spare flight suit and walked out to the parking lot. He checked the pistol in his shoulder holster as he got in his car, and sped off to Nikki's apartment. He had to get them out of Nexus right away. He knew Charon had a lot of enemies, and finding out who put the hit on him was going to take time. Time that he didn't have.

For now, every mid-level district boss under Charon would work together to find his killer, but their loyalty only went so far. Jase suspected that Charon's assassination was a play for control over Fluture by one of them and more blood would be spilled...especially his since he was closest to Charon.

He now faced an uncertain future. His dream of peace for the last year of his life was slipping away, but absolution was still within reach.

Jase parked in front of the apartment complex, ran to Nikki's room, and banged on the door. "Open up, Ms. Wells, it's me, Jase."

Nikki opened the door and he walked in hurriedly. She already had her flight gear on.

"What's wrong, Jase?" Nikki asked as she locked the door behind him.

"Ladies, it's time. I need you to get your things together." Jase handed Summer the flight suit. "Put this on, little one." He nodded and turned to Nikki. "The Zephyr is being fueled as we speak."

"What about my partner? Is he here?"

"Not yet, but he may still make it before you depart. If it came to it, can you fly that ship without a copilot?"

"I'm not leaving without him." Nikki glared as she helped Summer suit up.

"I'm afraid we may not have much of a choice." He turned to look at Summer. "Someone killed Charon early this morning. In the next hour, every district boss will be in Cybelle for a sit down and things could get ugly."

Jase grabbed their two bags and headed for the door. "We'd better get going." He said calmly.

They sat in silence in the car as Jase sped back to the hanger. He glanced at the rearview and could see that Summer was scared.

"I'll start my preflight when we get there." Nikki said. "It shouldn't take too long."

"Excellent." Jase smiled thinly. "Don't worry little one," he looked at Summer's reflection, "you'll be okay. You'll soon be free from Nexus."

"What will happen to you, Jase?" Summer asked glumly.

"Don't worry about me," he responded dryly, "I've got matters to tend to." He parked the car and got out briskly. "Hurry, we haven't got much time."

They walked quickly into the hanger as Doolie and his crew were clearing their equipment off the floor. The air was thick with tension and everyone was getting jumpy.

"Alright Ms. Wells," Jase smiled as he shook Nikki's hand, "I've done all I can, it's all on you, now." He looked at Summer and smiled. "Good luck with your life, little one." He turned and walked away.

"Jase, wait!" Summer ran to him and gave him a hug. "Thank you for everything." She whispered. "Thank you for your kindness. I'll never forget you."

"Be brave. It was an honor being your friend." Jase replied softly as he kissed her forehead and left.

Nikki gently grabbed Summer's arm and ushered her toward the Zephyr where Doolie was reviewing his checklist. "Stay close to me." She whispered.

"Good morning, Nikki." Doolie said a little too cheerfully as he looked up at the girls. "I think you'll find everything in order with your vessel. We're getting ready to tow her out of the hanger in a few minutes.

"Thanks for everything, Doolie." Nikki held her hand out.

"My pleasure, space jockey." Doolie nodded as he shook her hand.

"Let's get the preflight started..."

Scott accelerated to one hundred and thirty miles-per-hour and hit the cruise control. Thankfully oncoming traffic inbound to Fluture was nonexistent this morning. He lifted his shirt and looked at the extent of his injuries. The Tavara had definitely done a number on him with its claws. There were several deep gashes on his side still bleeding and there was nothing he could do about it now. He was in a world of hurt, but his wounds weren't fatal.

The sound of sirens startled him. He looked up into the rearview mirror and saw three police interceptors flashing their lights in pursuit. They were closing on him fast.

"Shit!" He cussed as he unzipped the backpack and rummaged with one hand as he steered with the other. He had six miles left to go and the heat was on.

Scott rolled the window down and grabbed one of the pyrogen grenades. He glanced back up and accelerated to one-sixty when he pulled the pin, dropped it out of the Avarno, and punched it to one-eighty.

He looked back in the rearview in time to see the frag detonate. The lead interceptor swerved to the left and rolled from the explosion as it was lifted off the road and slammed onto its side. The car tumbled and sent parts flying high into the air before it blew part and sent the other two interceptors into a spin. The second car came to a stop in the center median while the other flipped off the highway and came to a rest in a cloud of dust.

It wasn't enough. Scott could hear more sirens coming after him. Four more interceptors blazed through the smoking wreckage and were on his ass when he barreled into Cybelle at a hundred and sixty.

He raced through a four lane avenue that cut through an office area half-a-mile from the airstrip and was forced to slow down to eighty as he weaved through other drivers. Horns honked and cars skidded out of the way as he tore by them. The interceptors were right behind him the whole time.

Scott forced a couple of cars off the road when he careened off their sides and tore a panel off the SS-2. He smoked his brakes to avoid hitting a car in front of him; Scott cut a hard right to get past the swerving vehicle and saw the other driver give him the finger as he wheeled by.

"Fuck you too and the ground you walk on, cheesdick!" Scott growled through clenched teeth as he returned the gesture.

One of the squad cars pulled up to the passenger's side and started to side-swipe him. Scott hit the brakes and jerked the steering wheel a hard right and slammed into the interceptor's side. The squad car smashed into a row of parked cars along the boulevard and spun as another interceptor t-boned him and they both came to an abrupt stop as other cars screeched and plowed into them.

He saw the main parking lot entrance to the strip and veered into it. The SS-2 fishtailed and slammed into some parked cars as he punched it and accelerated toward the hanger where the Zephyr was sitting. He started laughing loudly as he thought about how badly this was going to end.

Scott gunned the sedan and forced a security guard to dive out of the way as he smashed through the swing gate and skidded on to the maintenance road that ran behind the hangers. The sirens wailed.

He drove down the side of the hanger and spun the Avarno sideways to a complete stop just outside the open bay doors where the Zephyr was sitting.

Scott grabbed the backpack and Trinity as he opened the driver door and rolled out onto the pavement. Squad cars screeched to a stop forty feet away from him as police troopers took cover behind their vehicles with their weapons drawn.

Scott took the Kirsten Auto and fired a controlled burst that riddled several interceptors and forced the officers to keep their heads down. They returned fire with a volley of rounds that thunked heavily against the SS-2 and shattered its windows. He looked to his right and saw Nikki with another girl duck for cover...

We were in the middle of the avionics check when we heard the sirens outside.

Doolie stopped and shot me a puzzled look. "Sounds like trouble." He said with concern as he looked out the bay doors.

"Yeah, and it sounds like they're heading our way."

"We'd better finish this up, Nikki."

We started to run the list again. Summer gazed at the Zephyr with awe as we walked to the back next to the cargo ramp.

"Nice job with the vertical stabilizer, Doolie."

"Thanks. That was one of the easier repairs. The fiber optics were the real challenge."

"Your ship looks fast, Nikki." Summer smiled.

"She's a good rig."

The sirens were just outside the hanger when we were startled by a sedan that screeched to a smoking halt outside. I saw Scotty roll out the door, crouch behind the damaged car, and start firing at the police cruisers that skidded to a stop across from him.

"Scotty! What the hell is going on?" I shouted as I watched in horror.

"Get in the ship and get out of here, Nikki!" Scott yelled as bullets sparked off the car.

"What about you?"

"I'll catch up," Scotty shouted as he picked up a rifle and took aim. "Fire-up the Zephyr, I'll be there in a second!"

Scott fired the rifle and a squad car exploded. The morning erupted with muzzle flashes as the police opened up with automatic fire.

Bullets ricocheted off a panel above my head and Doolie collapsed as he took a stray round in the head.

"Doolie!" I screamed. "Oh Shit! Get inside the ship, Summer!" I pulled out the Cobalt and squeezed off a few rounds. One of the police troopers peeked around the front of an interceptor and fired a burst that tore up the wall behind us.

Summer screamed as she put her hands over her head and curled into a ball as debris flew everywhere. I grabbed her arm and pulled her to her feet. "Come on, girl, we need to get out of here!" We ran up the Zephyr's ramp and through the cargo hold.

The forward bulkhead door slid open and I pulled Summer over to the flight panel and pushed her into the copilots seat.

"Strap in!" I ordered as I sat down and flipped the toggles that initiated the start-up sequence. "So much for the preflight."

The overhead console lit up as the critical flight systems enabled, and I started a systems check as I engaged the HUD in my helmet. The VDU screen lit up and I charted our coordinates to Earth. The Zephyrs burners ramped to ten percent thrust and quickly increased to twenty.

I handed Summer a flight helmet, she looked terrified and sat frozen in her seat as she stared out the canopy at the firefight outside.

"SUMMER! Put on the helmet!" I yelled sharply.

She snapped out of her daze and fumbled with the brain bucket, but she managed to slip it on.

I could hear the sharp rattle of automatic fire as Scotty faced-off with the cops. I disengaged the brakes and we started to roll forward...

Jase showed up with a group of men carrying automatic weapons. They ran for cover in the hanger as they fired on the police.

The sound of more sirens pierced the air as police reinforcements arrived at the scene and squad cars formed a barrier along the side of the bay doors. The stand-off had escalated into a full blown siege as law enforcement clashed with Charon's men.

Bullets shredded workstations in the hanger and several barrels full of chemicals exploded and killed two of Charon's men.

Smoke from the chemical fire rose to the structural steel supports of the hanger as Jase ran hunched over toward the riddled Avarno and slid painfully next to Scott. He crouched behind the chassis as rounds pounded the car.

"It's about time you got here, Mr. Scott." Jase coughed.

"Sorry about the car, Jase." Scott ejected a spent magazine from the Kirsten and slapped in a fresh clip.

"Why are the police after you? Did you rob a reserve?"

"I refused to pay a parking violation, and now they're a little upset with me. Do you always have this many men onsite?"

Another one of Charon's men stood up from behind a tool cabinet and fired at the cruisers with a sustained burst.

"Eat this you sons-of-bitches!" He screamed at the top of his lungs like a madman as he sprayed the barricade of interceptors. "Die you motherfuc..." He was blown apart when two troopers leaned out behind their cover and simultaneously opened up with assault shotguns.

"They've got Jackhammers!" Jase yelled back to his men. He looked at Scott and shook his head. "This is hopeless. We can't win this."

Scott looked over his shoulder when he heard the Zephyrs engines fire-up and the navigation lights on the wings blinked. He could also hear another firefight going on in the parking lot.

"We're surrounded, Jase!" Scott quickly leaned over, fired three shots, and dropped back behind the Avarno.

"Why are you doing this? What do you care if we live or die?" Scott asked harshly.

"I've got a business to run. Inviting the police to this facility isn't conducive to our operations." Jase replied sarcastically.

"There's one way to put an end to this mess." Scott glared as he reached into the backpack and pulled out a small device.

"I'm open for suggestions."

"I rigged this car with plastic explosives." Scott held up the transmitter. "I push this button and the blast will be powerful enough to kill god."

The Zephyr began rolling forward through the smoke and Scott could feel the heat from the ships thrusters deflecting off the back wall as tables and crates were sent tumbling across the floor from the jetwash.

The fire was spreading in the hanger, and muzzle flashes blinked from every direction as Charon's men stubbornly held their ground in the chaos.

"You need to get on that ship." Jase pulled out his pistol and flicked off the safety.

"You and your men need to get out of the hanger before I blow the car!"

"Can you do it from inside the ship?"

"Yes, but the transmitter has a three hundred meter range...the explosion will probably take out most of the airstrip along with the hangers and control tower. I'll have to detonate it when we're almost airborne." Scott slapped his neck when a round splintered off the pavement and sent fragments into his skin. "With a little luck we'll be within range to set it off, but you need to get the hell out of here or you'll get vaped."

"We don't have time for luck, Scott. Your plan has too many holes in it." Jase glowered.

"You got a better idea?"

"Give me the transmitter," Jase frowned. "I'm afraid it's going to take time to get my people out of here. I'll set it off when you're off the ground."

Scott hesitated then handed Jase the device. "It's your ass, Jase. I hope you know what you're doing. This thing is going to wipe this place out."

"Go!" Jase ordered.

Scott lobbed two pyrogen frags with one hand and ducked as they exploded and overturned three squad cars. Chunks of concrete rained everywhere as he got up and ran for the ramp.

"Cover fire!" Jase barked as he kneeled up and started shooting at the troopers. The rest of his men got up and charged the police line with their guns blazing.

Jase was knocked backwards when a round punched through his chest and splattered his face with blood. He slammed against the pavement and rolled face down as the transmitter popped out of his hand and landed a few feet away. The sound of machine gun fire reverberated in his ears...hollow and distant...

He looked up weakly and everything seemed to be moving in slow motion; muzzle flashes flared as bullet casings suspended themselves in mid-air, faces froze in fear as the chemical fire danced up the walls...

...his vision blurred as he saw Scott leap onto the Zephyrs retracting cargo ramp...he watched the ship taxi rapidly down the airstrip then blacked-out...

I could see the swarm of police interceptors from my vantage point as we rolled past them and steered toward the airstrip. I heard some explosions and thought our thrusters were malfunctioning until I saw some squad cars flip over and burst into flames

Scotty was nowhere in sight, but I had to keep the ship moving. I started closing the rear cargo ramp as we accelerated. I looked over control panel to confirm the navigational and cryogenic systems were go. The AGL's were also good, and the O2 generators began to prime the ship once the ramp sealed shut and locked-in.

The bulkhead door for the cockpit hissed open and Scotty staggered into the bridge and collapsed.

I lifted my visor and looked over my shoulder. "Scotty! Are you okay?" I shouted as I kept an eye on the runway. His filthy clothes were drenched in blood and he was out of breath.

"Go faster, Nikki," he said weakly as he looked out the canopy, "get us out of here!"

"You need to get your suit on, please tell me you didn't space it in your hotel room."

"Nikki, I'm old, not senile."

"Don't be a wiseass. Get your suit on and strap in!" I ordered as we reached the end of the airstrip and I turned the Zephyr a hundred and eighty degrees into the wind.

Scotty pulled his suit out of his backpack and struggled to get in it.

"Summer, you need to help him!" I said urgently, we've got less than two minutes until we're powered for lift-off."

Summer removed her helmet and ran to Scotty. She helped him get his arms into the gear and I heard Scotty groan in pain.

"Punch that button on the wall to your left." I instructed as the engines whined into a high pitch. A jumpseat folded down, and Summer helped Scotty buckle in.

"That hurts like hell." Scotty coughed as he leaned back and closed his eyes. "I don't suppose your ship has a stasis pod?"

"The e-pod in the cargo bay, but you'll have to wait 'til we're spaceborne."

"Summer, get back in your seat. We're ready to roll." I looked down the runway and took a deep breath. I gave the consoles another look as the thrusters roared.

I disengaged the brakes and the Zephyr lurched forward and rapidly accelerated.

"Next stop, Earth." I turned and winked at Summer as I held the control yoke. I reached down and pushed the levers on the center console forward as we were pushed into our seats by the g-forces.

The Zephyr barreled passed the control tower three-quarters of a mile down the strip when I put the thrusters in full afterburn, pulled back on the yoke, and brought her nose up...

———————

Jase opened his eyes and coughed. He felt like he had a tremendous weight on his chest and he had a hard time breathing. His vision was starting to blur and he could hear the sharp pops of gunfire around him.

He saw the transmitter on the ground just out of reach. He slowly pulled himself across the pavement and groaned as a searing pain consumed his body and made his muscles involuntarily tighten up.

He coughed and shuddered and felt himself cringe as he noticed he was lying in a growing pool of his own blood. His clothes were soaked with it.

Jase reached out and grabbed the device. The pain was unbearable. He didn't know how long he was unconscious and wondered if the Zephyr had made it out yet. He looked up and saw the police advancing on the hanger as they fired their weapons.

A body fell next to him, eyes glassy and lower jaw missing.

He heard the sound of thunder and looked up to see the Zephyr speed by and lift off the runway. He watched the ship ascend into the blue sky in a steep climb as the troopers overran the facility.

"You're free now, little one." He whispered and smiled. "We're both free."

Jase pressed the button and the world went silent...

Chapter 13

I retracted the landing gear as we climbed away from Cybelle. Suddenly, a jagged white light rippled across the sky and shook the Zephyr we rose above the mining sites and cleared the mountain ranges.

We were pushed against our seats as we hit Mach 4 and gained altitude over Nexus.

"Scotty, how are you doing?" I asked. When he didn't answer, I looked over my shoulder as saw that he had passed out.

I saw a thick dark cloud in the distance. It was huge and had to be at least fifteen or twenty miles long and a mile high. I looked at the scanner and it was defined as a solid mass moving across the sky.

"What is that?" I asked aloud as I stared at the strange undulating cloud.

"Butterflies." Summer said softly as she turned her head and looked at me.

"What?"

"Those are butterflies. Every five years they come home to Fluture."

"Incredible. Take a good look at them, Summer. They're the last you'll see of Nexus."

Summer looked on silently as we watched the butterfly migration dancing in the morning light, thousands of fragile wings fluttered blue like brilliant jewels.

The terrain vanished as we ascended into the high cloud banks. She lowered her head and cried quietly.

"Thank you, Nikki."

I smiled as I tipped the Zephyr's nose up and the sky darkened as we punched through the ionosphere.

"We'll going hypersonic as soon as we clear Nexus' gravitational pull. Then we're only six days from Earth."

"I didn't know your planet was that close."

"It's not. Summer, there's something you need to know about our journey…"

———————

When we stabilized in deep space, I engaged the auto-pilot and Summer helped me tend to Scotty's injuries with the medi-pac. He had lost a lot of blood from the nasty lacerations, but he seemed alert.

"We need to get the suit and shirt off, Scotty. Summer, can you grab that bag over there?"

"Go easy, I think my wounds finally stopped bleeding."

"What's left of your shirt is soaked." I tossed it aside, took a wet rag, and wiped the dried blood and grime off his upper body as his wounds started bleeding again.

"Geez, what happened to you?" I gasped as I used some steri-pads to clean his forearm and abdomen. "Any gunshot wounds?"

"No, I'm not shot. Long story, Nikki." He grimaced as he bit his lower lip. "Shit that stings!"

"Sorry about that. I've got just what you need, hang on." I stood up and went to the cargo bay. I opened the container with the whiskey, grabbed a bottle, and brought it back to the bridge.

"Here, this will take the sting off." I opened the bottle and handed it to Scotty, "Go ahead, take a slug."

Scotty nodded with a smile. "Cheers." He took a long swig and lay back against the wall.

"Give me some of that, I could use a drink myself." I grabbed the bottle and took a shot. "So, you were saying you had a story. Well, I'm all ears."

Summer gave me a puzzled look. "All ears?"

"Just an expression from home." I grinned. "Who did this to you, Scotty?"

"I'll give you the condensed version." Scotty groaned as he sat up. "I was hunting in the mountains the other day, and on my way back to camp, I was attacked by a Tavara pack. As you can see, they tore me up pretty bad. Barely made it out of there in one piece."

"Hunting is illegal in Icarus." Summer gave him a wary look.

"You went to Nexus to poach?" I asked doubtfully as I took out an injector and popped an anesthelogical cartridge into the casing and began to administer the local painkiller.

"Can you hand me that?" I asked Summer as I pointed at a stainless steel instrument in the kit.

"Yeah, I was hunting illegally," Scotty took a deep breath and clenched his hands into fists as I began to seal the flow of blood with a medical cauterizer, "you might say things didn't go exactly as planned."

"Am I supposed to believe that's why so many cops were chasing you?"

"As I told you before, the less you know about me the better off you are." He coughed as he took another drink. "This is really good hooch."

"Uh-huh. Back to working that sorry-ass "mysterious stranger" act again, I see." I shook my head as I sutured the wounds closed.

"Have it your way, Scotty." I winked as I smeared antibiotic ointment around the abrasions, and we bandaged him up.

"Here, take these for the pain." I handed him a couple of pills. "They'll help fight infection and make you sleepy too."

"Nice job, Nikki."

"What do you want me to do with this?" I held up the weapon he brought onboard with him.

"Careful with that, it's a Kirsten Automatic."

"Hunting, huh?" I chuckled.

"Just put it in my pack." Scotty said thinly.

"We're done here." I exhaled in relief. "Let's get you into the e-pod, we've got a ways to go before we get to the Pipe, and you need the rest."

———————

Scotty woke up two days later and joined us on the bridge. It was good to see him moving around and he was recovering nicely. He seemed to be in high spirits and his appetite was voracious, unfortunately, he was limited to FFR's and vitapacks to satisfy his hunger.

Summer's mood was also lighter considering she left everything behind in Fluture. It seemed like a great weight had been lifted from her shoulders now that she was starting over with her life.

I got to know her better as the days passed and she told me the story of her life in Nexus. I was impressed by her ability to adopt and survive a lifetime of abuse and overcome an addiction that brought ruin to so many people.

She was an incredible and courageous girl, proud and strong, and I was glad our lives crossed paths.

She was moving on, and so was I. Behind the innocence of her youth was the heart of a warrior; a girl that wouldn't give up hope, and a girl that would fight to keep her dreams alive. We decided to stick together for a while when we got back to Earth. We would help each other put the pieces of our lives back together.

Our friendship is just one of those things that I've come to consider a gift from fate. She and I came from such different upbringings but somehow a thread had pulled us together. It's like we were meant to be friends, and even the light years couldn't put the distance between us.

Scotty remained a mystery to me. There was still a side of his personality that remained hidden and dark, but all I had to do was look into his eyes and the whole story was right there. I managed to get one look in when we were in Cybelle, and it was like looking at the floor of an ocean; shadowy, unpredictable, and desolate.

We braced ourselves as I ramped the drives to full capacity and headed into the void of the Event Horizon. We were going home at last...

Epilogue

Suspected Crimelord Found Dead

By Jacob Fry | The Metropolitan   June 29, 2408

NEXUS (The Metro) – Robert Charon, age 54, of New Detroit, Earth was found dead in his country home on Sertina's Pass on Nexus yesterday morning at approximately 5:30am. Local law enforcement officials suspect Charon's death was the result of a power struggle within the infrastructure of the crime family that Charon allegedly led.

In a similar incident, twelve police troopers and fifty-eight people were killed in Cybelle the same morning during a violent stand-off with organized crime bosses believed to be linked with Charon.

The conflict resulted in a massive explosion that rocked the mining colony and injured over two hundred people and caused an estimated 18 million credits in damage to the colony's Inter-port and support buildings.

Emergency Response and HAZMAT Teams were onsite fighting a chemical fire caused by the explosion, and injured colonists were evacuated by air to Fluture General for treatment.

Police believe that Charon's killer is still at large, and detectives are still looking for leads.

Kurlie stood up and polished-off his drink. It was late, and the club was finally quiet. He looked across the dance floor as he put on his jacket and dashed the ashes of his cigar into the tray. He could hear the faint clatter of rain outside, and he put on his trench coat and checked the Gemini 9mm in his shoulder holster.

"Get the counts right, Charlie," he nodded at the bartender as he puffed on his stogie, "and lock up for the night."

"You got it, boss."

"Alright, then," Kurlie winked, "I'll see you tomorrow." He motioned at the two bodyguards that stood at the door waiting, and the three men went out the rear exit into the alley behind the tavern.

The driver had his car was idling in the rain and he turned to one of his men as he opened the back door of the sedan. "Stay here and help Charlie close."

The henchman looked at Kurlie vacantly and coughed a thick glut of blood before he collapsed.

"Jesus!"

Kurlie looked up and saw his other guard sprawled on the pavement. The silhouette of well-dressed figure holding a weapon with a sound suppressor stepped out of the shadows and stood quietly in the falling rain in front of him.

"YOU!"

"It's nice to be remembered. Good evening, Mr. Montrell."

"How the hell did you slip by my men at the Inter-port?"

"It's nice to see you again."

"Okay, let's get this over with." Kurlie growled as he pulled the Gemini out and pointed it at the man.

Scott pulled the trigger of the Raven and blew the 9mm out of Montrell's hand.

Kurlie turned to run when Scott fired two rounds into Montrell's legs and dropped him to the ground. Kurlie panted as he pulled himself across the asphalt.

He looked up and Scott stood less than three feet away...his eyes gleamed in the darkness, and his face was expressionless as he glared at Montrell.

"Who are you, you son-of-a-bitch!" Kurlie screamed as he shivered in the downpour.

"Holly." Scott pointed the Raven at Montrell's head and put two bullets between his eyes.

The rain fell harder as the man vanished into the haze.

Acknowledgements

A special thanks and shout-out across the pond to the following ladies for contributing their talents and beauty to the cover art, and giving a face to Nikki Wells:

Photography by Kate Monica for the image "pale":

http://fiery-sky.deviantart.com/

Vicky (model):

http://notwhatyouwanted.deviantart.com/

Other works by Anthony Hartig:

<u>ebooks/Kindle</u>:

100 Days From Home Book 1: Hard Rain

100 Days From Home Book 2: The Fall of Because

<u>Hard Copy</u>:

100 Days From Home 3rd Edition

(Complete work with 1 Bonus chapter)

 I grew up in Honolulu, Hawaii where a substantial portion of my youth was spent running around the streets of Waikiki with my friends. We did our best getting in trouble as we mixed it up with locals and tourists, and blowing Friday and Saturday nights being chased through the crowds by shady characters that we managed to piss-off with the wise-assed attitudes that only comes with that naive mindset of being indestructible.

I eventually moved to the mainland at the tender age of 17 where I attended Arizona State University in the early '80's. During my second semester as a sophomore I became one of the few undergrad instructors on campus for a Psychology course known by Psych majors as "Rat Lab"; a class that taught the basic Skinnerian principles of radical behaviorism.

In 1993 I met the girl of my dreams and married her two years later. I currently reside in the southwest with my wife/heroine and daughter (a tiny tornado with the face of an angel) where we live a quiet life in the suburbs with two cats named Mochi and Miko.

For more about the author visit:
http://100daysfromhome.co.nr/